SHATTERED HAND

Sarah's Secret War

J D Liddle

ISBN: 1507731620
ISBN 13: 9781507731628

CHAPTER 1

1863, OUTSIDE GETTYSBURG

In the early twilight, Sam Miller, a Union courier in the Army of the Potomac, was traveling southeast on a little-known country road. He was using a crude map to navigate back to the large Union army camp a dozen miles to the south of Gettysburg, Pennsylvania. Before the sun went down, he had seen a large dust cloud in the distance. That indicated a large force, but now that it was dark, he could not be sure of the direction. He hoped the lane he was on would turn out to be the correct road, but he could not be entirely sure.

The battle of Gettysburg in July of 1863 should have never been fought, at least not in that place. In spite of strong statements by the new Union commander about seeking the Confederate army and offering aggressive battle, General Meade had chosen a defensive strategy and began to lay out his lines about twelve miles south of the small Pennsylvania town. He hoped that Robert E. Lee would accommodate him by attacking him in his prepared position. General Lee, on the other hand, was not sure where the main Union army was located because his normally reliable cavalry commander, J. E. B. Stuart, had been out of touch with him for over a week. By this time, in the long march north through Maryland and into Pennsylvania, the eyes of the cavalry were critical to General Lee's strategy.

As a result of this strategy and confusion, a battle was brewing that neither commander wanted nor was ready for. By the eve of the battle, General Lee had sent couriers to notify his three corps commanders to march their troops to Gettysburg, even though this involved ordering General Early to backtrack from Harrisburg, where he was ready to attack the state capital. Commanders from both the North and the South had been dispatching patrols and couriers throughout the day and into the late afternoon and evening. They were all, in their own ways, trying to organize a battle that suited their styles of fighting, but it was like a colossal game of blind man's bluff.

Now, after traveling for two hours in the dark, Sam could still hear sporadic gunfire at his back as Union and Confederate patrols stumbled into each other in the night. He hoped that he would soon come on a picket line or some friendly patrol that could lead him where he needed to go. In the dark, he could hear what sounded like a child crying, and he headed for the sound. As he neared the sound, he realized that it was a woman weeping. He had never heard such a heartbroken cry before. As he slowly approached, he recognized in the dark a young woman seated on the ground, cradling the shoulders and head of a fallen soldier.

Apparently, the young woman was not aware of his approach, as she was not at all distracted from the young trooper whom she was tending. Sam stopped his horse just short of her, dismounted, and walked slowly toward her side, trying to quietly call out to her to let her know that he was approaching.

The young woman finally looked up at him, and with tears streaming down her cheeks, she said words that he would never forget. "Why did he need to die like that? Attacked from behind and murdered." Then she held up her left hand as if trying to block a blow. Sam was immediately alarmed by the appearance of the girl's mangled hand.

He was also shocked to realize that he knew the girl. She was from southeastern Tennessee, the daughter of a man by the name of Ted Clarke who had guided him, his father, his brothers, and their friends on a hunting trip in the mountains east of Cleveland, Tennessee, in 1860, just before the war began.

"Sarah, what are you doing here?" he asked as gently as possible.

CHAPTER 2
1860, CLEVELAND, TENNESSEE

Sarah Clarke was born on a farm just outside Cleveland, Tennessee, shortly before the war with Mexico. While her father was away fighting in that war, her mother, who was part Cherokee, died of a fever. Sarah was only three, so her father's sister, Mary, raised her until her father returned from the war, and then the two of them raised her until she was eleven or twelve. When her aunt married and moved to Knoxville with her stingy banker husband, Herbert Southwell Krantz Ewing, Sarah was left in the care of her father and two women whose husbands were helping him on his farm. Her aunt had taught her as many domestic skills as she could and taught her to read when she was very young using the family Bible.

They lived on a large farm where her father bred, raised, and trained mules. He was known throughout the region for raising the finest mules and skillfully training them to work. He was also a skilled hunter and guide, and he loved to teach Sarah all that he knew. From an early age, Sarah admired him for his gentle strength and cheerful countenance. Whenever he corrected her, he always ended by giving her a squeeze and saying something like, "It's OK. We'll both do better next time."

Ever since she could walk, Sarah was allowed to play in the yard around their house with her pet duck and small dog. Ted, her father, didn't have much time for the yappy dog, but Sarah loved him and the duck. She was amused when the small dog would take off after the duck until the duck got tired of the chase and started nipping at the dog, which would usually end the fun for one day.

By the time she was four, Sarah had started to notice the buildings and animals beyond the yard in the farm, and what's more, she had started to smooth small patches of dirt and use a stick to draw what she saw. Mary noticed that she had a sense of space and proportion, which surprised her. Sarah would draw anything she saw—even, on one memorable day, a picture of an amorous donkey and a mare.

"Don't you think that Sarah is a little young to be drawing mating animals?" Mary asked that evening.

Ted looked up surprised. "What do you mean?"

Mary took him to Sarah's drawing, lighting it dimly with the small lantern she had brought. "She drew this today."

Ted looked closely, and with a twinkle in his eye, he said, "She really is good with detail. But I don't think she will draw it again until she sees it."

When Sarah got a little older, she went to school in Cleveland whenever there was a teacher who happened to stay long enough to hold school. So she had as much formal education as any person of her age in a part of the country that was still more frontier than settled. She wanted to go to school more because of the chance she had on those occasions to use pencil and paper. It was a rare treat to draw something that would not be erased by someone walking through her small drawing patch in the yard or be ruined by wind or rain.

On Sarah's eighth birthday, Ted gave her a tablet of paper and a pencil that she cherished more than any gift she had ever received. One day she was headed for the back of the barn to draw a favorite mule when she came upon a scene she could hardly comprehend. One of the women who helped in the house, Elizabeth Smith, was behind the barn, a big cigar in her mouth, puffing as hard as she could. Sarah was startled but not nearly as surprised as Lizzy at the unplanned meeting.

They stared at each other for what seemed like an hour, and finally Lizzy said, "My father used to smoke these before he died, and anytime I have a chance, I smoke one, and it helps me remember him."

"Does it taste as bad as it smells?" Sarah asked, waving her hand in front of her face to try to get rid of the smell.

"Oh, you get used to it. But the first time I smoked a whole one, I was sick for about a week."

"It looks so big. It must take a long time to smoke."

Just then Lizzy looked at Sarah and realized that she had her pencil and pad of paper with her. Then she made a big mistake by saying, "Don't you go drawing me now. I don't need to be embarrassed by something your father could see."

Sarah probably would not have thought of trying to draw Lizzy because she used her paper so carefully. But now, the seed was planted, and the harvest would come in due time. Lizzy was right to worry about the skill that Sarah already had in depicting detail.

Lizzy had watched Sarah since her husband, Oliver Smith, (Smitty) had been hired to help with the farm, and she with some of the housework. They were given living quarters in a small cottage on the farm as part of the arrangement and so had been around the family from as early as Sarah could remember. In fact, Lizzy had presumptuously scolded Ted on many occasions because he doted on Sarah's wants as much as he possibly could. "You're going to spoil that child terrible, and then there will be hell to pay," she repeated at least once a week. Ted regularly ignored her as he went about his business and didn't let it bother him any more than he did the advice offered by Smitty, on how to manage his farm.

The immediate result of the meeting behind the barn came the same evening while Ted and Sarah sat in front of the fireplace. He was smoking a pipe, and Sarah was carefully sketching him with the smoke curling up around his head as he peacefully contemplated the fire. He was lost in thought about the loss of his young wife and what he would do in the future. She got his attention and showed him the picture she had drawn of him. He turned the page over and started to laugh.

"What's so funny?" she asked.

"Is this a picture of a bride you have picked out for me?" he asked, then laughed some more as he gazed at Sarah's drawing of a lanky woman with long arms, smoking a big cigar.

Of course, it was the picture of Lizzy that she had warned Sarah not to draw.

There were single young women in and around Cleveland that took an interest in the widower and his daughter, but Ted could not really imagine being close to anyone else while he was trying to raise Sarah. The girl seemed to constantly change, and she grew more like her mother every year. She now was starting to resemble the beautiful wife he remembered with long raven black hair and dark brown eyes. Sarah was not as deeply colored as her mother, but rather she had Ted's light olive complexion. He could not keep up with her maturing and would only marvel at each new accomplishment.

Sarah was very bright so her schooling came easily, and she was very competently running the household by the time she was ten. But she was far more interested in the farm and her father's work with the mules he bred. He had always told her that when she was ready, he would let her help train the mules. When Mary left, he thought it would be a good time to have Sarah begin helping with the horses, donkeys, and mules. He hired another couple to help with the house and the farm so that Sarah would have time to work with him and so that he could devote more time to her.

As he was raising the mules, he would always look for those pairs that would work well in teams because it would increase their value. He noted Sarah's interest in all that he did and so started to teach her as much as he could about breeding and pairing them from the time they were young.

Ted usually thought that the best way to team animals was by size and similar strengths, but Sarah instinctively knew that two mules of the same strength did not always work well together in a team. Ted observed as he started to have her work with the young mules that she had an instinct for the animals that he did not have. He looked upon them as mainly work animals, but he could tell that she loved them and saw their individuality more clearly. To him, they only varied in strength and willingness to work. Sarah could sense the mules' personalities. Some were more social, others loners; some were more protective, others inhibited, needing protection. Sarah would often point out to her father things like which mule would be good for plowing alone, or which one would be better for riding, or which two could work together because they pulled together and got along.

CHAPTER 3

1860, MOUNTAINS EAST OF CLEVELAND

Because Ted had great skills in tracking and hunting, he was contracted at least twice a year to lead hunting parties from the North into the Appalachian Mountains, men who came hunting for black bear and other trophy animals. Usually the parties consisted of wealthy men who were put in contact with Ted by his brother-in-law, Herbert, who generally went along on the hunts. Sarah usually went to stay with her aunt Mary while these hunting parties went out for two or three weeks. But the year 1860 was different. Sarah was now sixteen, and her father promised her that she could go on the hunt, in spite of the fact that her Aunt Mary was ready to have her first baby and wanted Sarah to help her when it was born.

Mary and Herbert were staying close to home to wait for the birth of their first baby, which would be born sometime between mid-October and mid-November. As a consequence (or benefit), Herbert would not be going along on this occasion.

Before the first big hunting party arrived, Ted decided to take Sarah out to look for bear sign and to make sure that their usual campsite was in good condition. Sarah had been hunting many times before, but only on short trips and only just the two of them and maybe one or two of the farm workers to help. This year, there would be more to do in preparing food and equipment because of the size of the group so Ted took along Smitty to help with the camp and hunt preparations.

The base camp was located in a small box canyon about fifteen miles east of Cleveland, the entrance to which was mostly hidden by trees and underbrush. Sarah's father had stumbled across it years before when he was hunting white-tailed deer and found that this was a favored nesting area for them.

They spent some time clearing areas where the tents would be set up and preparing a cache of firewood. They would camp here for the night, then spend two or three more days looking for bear sign, and then return home to meet the first hunting party.

There was one day that made her uneasy. On that day, whenever Ted and Smitty left her alone to find wood or check on the mules or do anything that separated them for even a short time, Sarah had the uncomfortable feeling that she was being watched. She took small comfort that Smitty was a little nearer the camp than Ted. She always felt safer with her father than with any other person. She knew that there were not many people who knew about this small box canyon, so she should not feel insecure. When her father came back from his last check of the trails, she mentioned her unease to him.

He did not want to worry her, but he had found human tracks at the entrance of the canyon that he did not recognize. He decided that they should not separate while looking for bear sign the next couple of days and that he would be more cautious in the areas where they looked.

He could not know by the look of the tracks that they belonged to two brothers, Clarence and Amos Taylor. Their father, Clifton Taylor, owned a small plantation just north of Chattanooga. Several years ago, they had discovered the grotto that Ted's party was using for their camp and since then had often checked it for wild game. The two young men had been watching the party, especially Sarah, wondering who they were and what they were doing.

That night, after Smitty, Ted, and Sarah had finished cleaning up after supper, they started to talk about the coming election and what Ted thought might happen if the North managed to elect Abraham Lincoln. The political leaders in South Carolina were the most outspoken about the dire consequences of that event and were already calling some state militias into service. Some of the more extreme leaders were talking about leaving the Union.

"They are already stirring the hornet's nest before anyone really knows who will be elected," Ted said. "It makes me think that they would like to leave the Union no matter what happens in November."

"What do you think they will do if Lincoln is elected?" Sarah asked.

"They are talking of secession."

"Why?"

"They talk about the federal government not having the right to impose any limitations on state laws. But as I see it, the only laws they really want to protect are those enforcing slavery. They have also insisted that the federal government impose slave-catching laws on nonslave states. Over the years, the compromises that have been worked out have mostly benefited slave owners, and I think they see Lincoln's election as the beginning of the end for those compromises."

"But I have friends whose families own slaves, and they treat them kindly. So shouldn't the laws protect them and their right to keep their slaves? According to my teacher in school, it's one of the rights of the states to decide laws governing property and how it can be used and taxed," Sarah said. "What would you do if the government came in and told us how to raise our work animals?"

"I see a great deal of difference in raising mules and keeping humans for slaves," Ted responded. "How would you feel if we were enslaved property and our owner, who was kind, died and left us as property to his heirs? Then, if his family needed money to pay debts or taxes, they would sell us. Being forcibly separated would break my heart," Ted said. "I have always felt that slavery is an evil that is corrupting our nation. I think that a lot of the slave owners are uncomfortable about the moral issues, and so they are talking about political rights instead of right and wrong."

Sarah thought about this for a few moments and realized she had never thought of slaves as having the same family feelings that she had. She had always considered slavery a necessary part of owning a plantation. Then she remembered that Ted's father had been a slave owner and that it had caused a bitter split between her father and grandfather when Ted was young. She had been told that when her grandfather died, Ted was away in Mexico fighting in that war, and he would not come home for the funeral. When the war was finally over and he came home from Mexico, he wouldn't even consider returning to help with the plantation, so it was sold off, and all of the proceeds went to his sister, Mary. "What do you think the people in the South will do if Lincoln becomes president?" she asked.

"From what they are saying and doing, I believe they mean to enforce their will, even if it comes to war. I worry that the more strident leaders in South Carolina will be able to talk a majority of leaders in their own and other Southern states to join with them and secede from the Union."

"If they do, what do you think will happen?"

"There are two possible outcomes. One, the leaders in the rest of the country will not want to force the issue and will let the Southern states leave the Union, or two, the people in the rest of the country will realize that it will sooner or later lead to war over issues of territory and slavery and so will fight to preserve the Union now."

"Who would control the territories that we bought from France and took from Mexico?" Smitty asked. "It seems that there would be a lot to fight about in the future."

"I think you have stated what the future would be, Smitty. You and I have seen war in Mexico and know how horrible it is. Think if there were to be a war here in the United States between brothers and friends. I believe it would be worse than anything we can now imagine."

"Do you think either side is right?" Sarah asked.

"Neither side is completely right because there have been so many compromises to preserve slavery over the years, but in my opinion, the time has come to face up to the issue and end it now. My father told me that when he was a young man, he thought that slavery would die of its own weight—and then the cotton gin was invented, which made it more profitable to use slaves. He even increased the number of slaves he owned because he could put more land into cultivating cotton. Then the will to end slavery became weaker and weaker in the South. Now if I understand correctly, the Republican party wants to legally limit slavery to the states where it now exists, but the Democrats are for more compromises and extending slavery into the western territories. The hard-line Southern leaders won't hear of limiting the boundaries of slavery because then they know that it could eventually end because there would be no new land to move slaves to, and any new states would be free, giving more power to free states."

Sarah knew that her father was leading up to something so she asked, "What will all this mean to us?"

"One of the men who will be with this next hunting party, Charles Murphy, has offered to buy or lease our farm. He says that he wants to give his son the experience of working on a farm and learning what it's like to work hard for a living. He is a rich man and is willing to pay a good price. I believe a good option would be to lease it to him and then see what happens. If it comes to secession and war, I would enlist in the army. I am willing to fight to make sure that the Union survives, and I hope it will bring an end to slavery."

"What if Tennessee elects to side with South Carolina and the other slave-holding states. Then you would be going against neighbors and friends. Even Aunt Mary and Uncle Herbert have some slaves that live with them and help on their property." Sarah was so distressed at the thought that her father might be making a mistake. He would surely end up fighting his friends. This came as a sudden shock to Sarah, and she couldn't help the tears that came immediately. She loved her life and home, but most of all, she didn't want her father to go away into danger. "If you leave and the farm is leased, where will I go?"

"I have written to Mary, and she has agreed to have you come and live with them. We may both be there for a time because the future is so uncertain. I know this is sudden, but I wanted to talk with you before anything was decided."

"It sounds like you have already decided a lot without telling me, and besides, Uncle Herbert always makes me feel small."

"I know Herbert can be difficult to get along with and that he makes you feel uncomfortable, but I can't help how I feel about the Union and slavery. When I fought in the war in Mexico and became friends with men from all over the country, I came to feel strongly that we should have abandoned slavery long ago. Men from the North talked about immigrants who came to this country without education or money, but who nevertheless, by their hard work, made something of their lives. I believe that Negro men and women who have been held as slaves deserve the chance to do the same thing."

Sarah could not sleep very well that night thinking of all the reasons she and her father should stay on the farm no matter what happened in the country. She wanted to convince her father not to go, but she did not know how to argue with his experience and wisdom. She had never before considered that her world could change so much overnight.

The next day they finished preparing the site and then started to look for bear signs in the mountains. The last thing they did was look for good sources of ripening berries so Ted and Smitty could construct a blind and add bait to the area where they would wait and watch for bears. When hunting bears, Ted didn't like to use dogs because of the confusion and danger they created. He had always been more successful looking for the most likely places bears would frequent and then wait for them to show up.

When they were satisfied that there were enough bears that could be hunted nearby, they returned to the farm to await the arrival of the party from Boston.

CHAPTER 4
1860, CLEVELAND, TENNESSEE

The hunters from Boston arrived a few days earlier than expected. The hunting party was a repeat group who had hunted with Ted a couple of years before. They had been so pleased with the first hunt that this year they brought a professional taxidermist. They wanted to make sure the bears would be skinned and the hides properly prepared for mounting and stuffing.

Ted and Sarah were surprised to see that the two men brought their four sons along, and other men to help with their camp. That made Ted uncomfortable about taking Sarah along on the trip. The four young men, who ranged in age from fifteen to twenty-one, were all very polite, but there was something about the situation that made him worry about how Sarah would feel. Would she be attracted to one of the sons, or would they make her feel small in any way because she was not from a wealthy family and was not from their type of "society."

There were other problems created by the size of the party, particularly about ensuring adequate food and shelter. They were heading into the mountains at a time of year when the weather was unpredictable and could change very quickly, so they would need more tents and enough food to last in an emergency.

There was an additional problem when Ted realized that the young men were not competent using the large muskets that were needed to bring down a bear. He and the fathers of the young men had a heated discussion about whether they would be allowed to carry and use the rifles. The older men decided to allow the young men go along on the hunts and carry the guns, but they would be forbidden to fire them until Ted had time to teach them how to use them and they showed not only competence but good sense in handling the weapons. This decision upset the young men, but Ted refused to lead the group if the fathers did not strictly enforce the rule. He made it clear that if there were any breach in the rule, the hunt would be abandoned, and he, his men, and Sarah would return home. The Bostonians could come with them or find their own way home; it did not matter to him.

There were a few days before they left for the mountains, and during that time, Ted took the time to start teaching the young men how to handle their muskets. He was especially careful to talk about safety and how to hold the large muskets when firing.

He also took Sarah aside and talked to her about going to stay with her aunt, that maybe she could help with the new baby if it came while they were on the hunt.

"I don't like Uncle Herbert, and besides, you promised that I could go on this hunt with you," Sarah reminded him.

"I really want to take you with me too, but I worry that you will be uncomfortable with no other women around."

"Why don't you ask Harry or Smitty to bring their wives? Then I could be with them, and they could help with the cooking," Sarah said.

"We have tonight and tomorrow to think about it. If I can get hold of another tent, and Harry and Smitty are willing, maybe we will do that," Ted answered.

With that, they went back to the work of putting together all of the food and gear they would need. That evening, Ted checked with Harry and Smitty and found that their wives were more than willing to go out on the hunt. Ted was able to find a tent that could accommodate Sarah and the other women, so he felt a little better about including her in the expedition.

Sarah was very aware of the young men, and they her. She was attracted to Chauncey and Martin. Chauncey was older, blond with striking blue eyes that seemed to see everything at once. He was taller than his friends and the only son of Charles Murphy. He was also a very observant young man and picked up the lessons in trail lore that Ted was teaching the young men. He and Ted seemed to form a quick bond.

Martin was the youngest of the group, just a year younger than Sarah. He was short for his age and, in fact, would never grow to stand more than five foot two inches in boots with the most generous heels. He was always smiling in a way that lent an elfish cast to his countenance. He was boisterous and quick-tempered, but he also had a fun sense of humor that manifested itself whenever he was able to play a practical joke on his older brothers. He was also a faster runner than any of his brothers, which made it possible for him to avoid a lot of the consequences of his teasing.

Sam was the oldest of the three sons of Samuel Miller, and he looked kind enough, but he was not handsome and would not have the same presence walking into a room as Chauncey or his own younger brother, Marvin. When Sarah tried to draw a picture of each young man, it was easy to capture Chauncey's and Marvin's handsome countenances because of their obvious charm. Marty was also easy because his smile was so natural and distinctive. Sam, on the other hand, frustrated her because she could never catch his face with any certainty. One day, after she had done her best, she looked closely at the result and quickly crumpled up the sheet of paper and threw it. The paper landed at Marty's feet as he was approaching her.

He picked it up smiling and asked if it was a love letter to him. "Open it up, and you will see how much I love you," she replied.

He looked at it. "You must really love me because you have drawn a picture of Sam." He handed her back the drawing.

"The roughness captures his features better. Maybe he will look better with more age," Sarah mused, and they both laughed.

To watch the young men together on the trail, one could not imagine that they had deep differences concerning their futures or what they hoped would happen to the country during the next few months. They obviously enjoyed being together and were competitive in many ways, especially when learning to shoot the muskets.

Chauncey had been convinced for some time that the federal government had no right to enforce its will on the states in any political matter. For him, it went much deeper than the present issues of slavery and what would be the law in the territories. In this, he and Sarah felt the same, and they talked about what might happen if Abraham Lincoln was elected in a few weeks. They both felt that any state had the right to leave the Union and either join with any other state or go it alone if that was what their people wanted.

Sam was ambivalent about the issues regarding federal and states' rights, but was a committed abolitionist. He had studied the life of the British reformer, William Wilberforce, and felt that the United States should have led in the struggle to end slavery instead of holding onto the old way of life for political expediency. After all, Thomas Jefferson had written in the Declaration of Independence that all men were created equal.

The middle son of Samuel Miller, Marvin, felt much the same as his older brother about slavery but was quiet and less vocal about his feelings. If Sam were part of any conversation about the near future, Marvin pretty well let Sam talk for him. If Sam wasn't around, he could be very eloquent in stating his personal feelings.

Marty didn't express any particular opinion but loved to get the other young men excited, talking about politics. Sarah noticed that whenever he did this, it was one of the few times he listened carefully, as if trying to make up his own mind from what they were each saying.

CHAPTER 5

1860, MOUNTAINS EAST OF CLEVELAND

Rebecca and Elizabeth, the wives of Harry and Smitty, were excited about the chance to travel with their husbands, even though it was a working trip. They would be mainly responsible for the cooking, which also meant drawing water from the small brook. But they would not put up with the men not doing at least some of the housekeeping in the camp, including washing dishes and keeping the fires going. They also inspected the men's tents during the days they were away from camp and made sure that the men and boys kept the cots and tents clean.

It was a three-day journey from Ted's farm to the little canyon in the Smokey Mountains where their party would make its base camp. The second day was particularly hard because of the initial climb into the mountains. Sarah had some problems with the two mules, Morgan and Theresa, her favorites, which she had hitched to her wagon and brought along on this trip. During one particularly hard segment, when the climbing was difficult because of the steep, rocky terrain, they were balky and nervous because Marty was walking so close to Morgan's side. When the group finally stopped for the evening, and the men were busy preparing the camp, Sarah took her mules off to a nearby brook to let them water and graze. When the mules finished, she started to rub them with a coarse towel and brush. While she worked, she busily talked to herself about how backward the boys from Boston were, how little they knew about the outdoors, and how poor their manners were. Suddenly, there was a noise behind her that startled her back into the moment.

She called out to see who was around but got no answer. At that moment, a dark shadow descended quickly over her, and she was trapped in a piece of rough cloth, held by strong arms. She did manage one well-aimed kick to a tender shin and then a stomp on the exposed instep of a light boot. The cry of anger and pain sounded very like the sound made by a small terrier she had once seen kicked by one of her mules. She realized as she was falling to the ground that her attacker had lost his grip and was now underneath her. Then she heard the overwhelming laughter of Chauncey, Sam, and Marvin who had put Marty up to trapping her to try to scare her.

Neither Sarah nor her attacker would admit to any fear, but she did start to laugh as Marty started to rub both his leg and foot at the same time trying to hold back tears of pain and frustration.

When dinner was cleaned up that evening and everyone was starting to prepare to sleep after a long day, Sarah and Marty started talking quietly. Sarah found herself drawn to Marty as she might be to a brother who had been hurt by bullies. He explained that the older boys had put him up to the earlier trick, and he was willing to go along because of the incident during the day when she had deliberately cracked her whip close to him to get him away from the side of the mules.

"Why did you crack that whip at me today?" he asked.

"You were making them nervous, and if I hadn't made you move away, Morgan would have kicked out at you. If you think my kick to your shins tonight hurt, think of Morgan's kick and how much more severe it would have been."

"How could she have kicked me when I was at her side?"

"You don't know much about mules, but I can tell you that they can kick almost as hard to the side as they do to the back. You are a stranger to them, and when they are working hard and annoyed by something or someone, they will start to kick and buck. That could have been disastrous today."

"You seem to love your mules more than you do people."

"No, there are times when I don't even like to be around them, but I recognize their nature and am able to anticipate some of their difficult ways. These two are my favorites though, and I do treat them better than a lot of the others we have raised."

"You call them Morgan and Theresa. I thought that maybe they were male and female but noticed that they are both females. Why is one named Morgan?"

"Her full name is Morgan le Faye. She was born when I was reading about King Arthur and his round table of knights. I thought the name suited a mule. In some ways, she lives up to the name. She seems to be a true witch around most of the other mules. Theresa is the only one she will work with in harness, maybe because she is younger and the daughter of the same mare."

Sarah was now getting tired and wanted to go to sleep, but Marty had one more question.

"If I get Chauncey to walk alongside Morgan, do you think you could get her to kick him? He has been giving me a bad time ever since we left Boston. He was really against Marvin and me coming on this trip, saying that we were too young and would only get in the way."

Sarah thought for a few minutes. "Maybe you should think of something else to do. I wouldn't want to take the chance of severely

injuring anyone. There must be a way to let him know that you deserve to be along on this trip."

Marty seemed disappointed at her response but let the subject
drop and went off to bed.

CHAPTER 6

1860, HUNTING CAMP

The days in the mountains were glorious this time of year with the nip of an early fall in the air and the colors of the trees so intense that Sarah wished that the trip would last a lot longer. She was finding out in different ways she enjoyed the company of the sons of the hunters.

Sarah was the only female who would be able to go out with the men each day and participate in the hunt. Chauncey and Marvin resented this, mainly because she had already shown that she was better with a rifle than they were. She could load faster and hit a target more consistently than they could. Neither Sam nor Martin was concerned that she could shoot better than they could. They were both happy to be along on the hunt and were taking advantage of the practice that they were involved in each day. Each day, the fathers and sons had a shooting competition with the winner getting to wear his red hunting shirt for the day. These were the special shirts that all would wear when the actual hunt started.

The first day of the hunt was rainy and colder and especially hard on the young men. They thought that the weather would hold for them and when they came back to camp in the evening, Marty was complaining bitterly that he had not even seen a bear. "I don't see why we didn't even get a shot at a bear. Why are we here?" he complained. "Maybe we should be higher up in the mountains. Why don't we try another location tomorrow?"

Finally, his father took him aside and said, "You insisted that you wanted to come along instead of staying behind in Boston. If you want to go home tomorrow, I will personally hire one of Ted's men to escort you back to Cleveland. If you keep on complaining, then I will take that as your answer, or you can go back to your tent and pack up."

Marty was stung by his father's rebuke and was very quiet for the rest of the evening. Sarah noted it as a rather pleasant change.

"Today we will divide our group," Ted said. "The first blind will be for Sarah, Marty, Marvin, Mr. Miller, and me. The second group will be Harry, Mr. Murphy, Chauncey, and Sam. Smitty, you will stay in camp and help until noon and then come up and replace anyone who is tired of the hunt."

Samuel Miller said, "Marty, we just need to be patient and wait for them. Today is warmer, and maybe you will at least see a bear."

Just before noon, Marty got his chance. He was just standing to change positions when a large male bear started to investigate the large cache of bait that was laid out that morning. The explosive shot he heard came from behind and off to his left. Mr. Murphy had seen the bear first and had fired.

"Did I hit him?" he yelled.

The answer was immediate and came from the slightly wounded bear. The shot had grazed its flank and had enraged the beast. It started toward the closest blind where Marty was standing exposed.

Another explosive shot rang out. The bear was only now about thirty yards away from Marty and coming fast. Chauncey had stood up just in front of his father. He had a lucky angle and perfect aim.

His shot hit the bear just behind the right shoulder. The bear was mortally wounded and dropped.

Before the hunt began, Ted had instructed the hunters, "If we are fortunate enough to bring down a bear, don't rush up to make sure that it's dead. We will all stay calm for at least a half hour to let it die. Then when I give the OK, we can all slowly and carefully approach."

"Chauncey, why don't you be the first to go look," said his father. "We will be right behind you with our rifles loaded, but since it was your shot, I think you should be the first to see."

Chauncey made his way slowly up to the bear, and Ted was right behind him. "That was a fine, calm shot, Chauncey. You may not know it, but you saved Marty and me from the bear's final charge."

The entire group looked at Chauncey with admiration, but he was strangely quiet. To think that he had killed something that large with just one shot was overwhelming to him.

Sarah watched his sensitive response closely and was drawn to his modesty.

That night around the fire the young men were now excited and telling each other about how they felt during the fearful encounter that day.

"Chauncey, all I can say is thank you for hitting him when you did," Marty said.

"If I had known it was you he was after, Marty, I would have been tempted to let him eat lunch first," Chauncey joked in return.

Ted said quietly, "I am just happy that we were all able to walk away and you young men responded so well to what you have been taught."

During the next ten days, they had a successful hunt, killing two more large male bears in their prime. Their hides would be cured and then eventually stuffed by the taxidermist. Ted would smoke the meat into a tough jerky that could be kept to eat during the winter. The process of smoking the meat would take time that Charles

Murphy and the Millers did not want to spend in the mountains. Sarah was to be sent with the hunting party and the wagon with the hides to guide the party back to the farm. She was to return for her father with enough supplies for him to finish making and packing the jerky.

The last evening around the campfire, the men talked about the mountains and all of the stories of lost travelers who had disappeared, never to be seen again. Smitty said that there was one person who kept reappearing even though she had been lost about seventy years before.

"She had been an indentured servant and left the home she was living in at Knoxville with a gambler who promised to take her east to Baltimore, then to New York. Instead of going east, they followed the mountains to the south and were last seen down around Chickamauga Creek. There was a trading post there, and the Frenchman who ran it was hunting in the mountains around here when he found the bloody remains of her clothing. He found a lot of bear tracks around the spot but no sign of the gambler.

"At night in the fall, hunters see shadows of a young woman leading a bear around the woods close to where they are camped. I know of at least two hunters who wandered away from their camp during the night and who were later found by their companions dead and partially eaten. Isn't that right, Ted?"

Ted looked up from his conversation with Mr. Miller and said, "I've heard those stories, but I don't have any reason to believe them."

"Well, I have known the hunters who told the stories and named their dead friends," Smitty said, "and I don't have any reason to doubt them. The bears get very hungry this time of year, just before their winter hibernation, and they will eat almost anything."

With that, Smitty got up and went to talk to his wife for a few minutes.

The young men were entertained by the story, but Sam said that he didn't believe in ghosts and certainly not one who would lead bears to where hunters were. Chauncey agreed and said that if he saw the ghost or bear, he would like to check them out with one of the big hunting rifles they had been using on their hunt.

It was late when everyone finally bedded down for the night, almost as if they were all reluctant to end the hunting trip that they had enjoyed so much. It would have been nice for each of them, for different reasons, not to have to return to civilization and the concerns and fears that they all had about the future.

In the middle of the night, the camp was suddenly awakened by the loud sounds of angry scuffling and laughter coming from the direction of the young men's tent. Sam, Marvin, and Chauncey were loudly cursing and then there was very loud, almost hysterical laughter coming from near their tent. By the time lanterns were lit and the fathers were at the tent calming down the boys, they were able to start piecing together what had happened.

Marty had gotten up about a half hour before and had retrieved a large piece of bark he stripped from one of the trees cut down for firewood. He chopped it into the rough form of a standing bear and placed it between a lit torch and the tent where his brothers and Chauncey were sound asleep. He then took some large branches and scratched at the sides of the tent while roaring as loud as he could and then screaming like a girl. When the boys suddenly awoke, they saw the shadowy form of a bear and heard a frightening noise. Their own yells and curses only added to the confusion, a confusion that peaked when they found out that Marty had tied all of their trouser legs together. In the confusion, their curses became louder, and Marty's laughter became even more hysterical. Each of the offended young men vowed to get Marty back at the earliest opportunity.

The next morning, the only thing said to all of the young men was that they had better be on their best behavior traveling back to Cleveland and that their fathers would be keeping an especially keen eye on them. They finished breaking down the camp and packing the wagons, and they were away by noon.

Ted spoke quietly to Lizzy about the return trip. "Will you keep an eye on Chauncey and Sarah? He's an attractive young man, and I am afraid she is infatuated with him."

"She is a lot smarter about these young men than you give her credit for, Ted. Maybe the best thing she has learned from the mules is how much they act like men," Lizzy responded. Then seeing the look on Ted's face, she added, "I'll watch just to see that there is no manipulation because of her young age, though."

"Thanks to the early kill, I won't need to stay here as long finishing up the jerky. I should follow in less than a week, right after we have cleaned everything up."

There was a certain amount of danger in Ted's decision to remain on his own. Some of the hill people would be out hunting for their supply of winter meat, and he knew that there were those who would not hesitate to attack him for both the meat and guns he carried. His only hope was that they would not be close by, and he could continue the smoking process without strangers taking notice. He reconsidered at the last minute though and had Harry stay with him. He sent Smitty along with the departing hunters, charged with seeing that the hunting party returned safely to Cleveland.

CHAPTER 7
1860, KNOXVILLE, TENNESSEE

Before the hunt started, Ted had signed the lease with Charles Murphy. When he arrived safely home, after saving as much of the bear meat as possible, he and Sarah started to pack the things they would take to Knoxville. They decided to leave the basic kitchen table and chairs, the bedroom furniture, and other odds and ends in the home. Their better furniture they decided to crate up and ship to Knoxville where they would either store it or find room for it in Mary and Herbert's home.

Sarah would miss the farm and the animals they were leaving more than the home. She decided to take her favorite mules, and Ted would take his best team to cart the few household furnishings that they would carry with them.

Leaving was harder for Sarah than she had anticipated. It was not quite the adventure she tried to convince herself it would be. The first day they only traveled five miles, and she felt that she was not really moving. The road was bad because of the weather, and so the trip took almost two weeks. Whenever they could, they would stop at a tavern or inn, but they were compelled to camp in the open some nights. The weather was cold, and this made Sarah feel even gloomier about the future.

When they arrived at her Aunt Mary's home in Knoxville, the welcome was warmer than she expected. Mary and Ted had always been close, but now Herbert was friendlier than he had ever been in the past. They lived in a large home that had more than enough room to accommodate Ted and Sarah and their household belongings.

Mary's baby was due any day now, and Sarah was very excited to be where she could see her new cousin come into her family. She often wondered how it would be to have brothers and sisters of her own. Her father had never taken the time to look for another wife, and she wondered why. She also felt the need on many occasions for a mother, even though she and her father were close. While she was with Mary, she intended to be as much help as possible around the house and with the baby.

Herbert seemed relieved that she was there, and she sensed that he knew that she intended to help Mary. Sarah loved being with Mary and her new baby, and true to her word, she did everything she could to help Mary. Ted was preoccupied with the elections that had taken place just before they arrived in Knoxville. He was very alarmed by the reaction in the South, especially that of South Carolina. He sent a letter to a friend from the Mexican war to ask him what he intended to do, if anything.

Ted heard back from his friend that he was joining a militia company in Pennsylvania. They did not have any real equipment, but they could drill and at least be as ready as possible for war, should it come. He invited Ted to come to Pittsburgh for a visit, and they could renew their friendship, which had developed in Mexico so many years before.

CHAPTER 8

1861, THE BAXTERS

The first week in February 1861, Ted and Sarah traveled by train north to Pittsburgh to meet his old friend. Ralph Baxter had a son, Ralph Junior, who was a year older than Sarah, and a daughter, Minnie, who was the same age as Sarah. Sarah didn't realize when she first met these new friends from a big city how close they would become over the next several years.

Ted and Ralph had been closer than brothers during the Mexican war, and when they saw each other again, it was clear had a bond only shared by people who have faced danger and tragedy together. They had saved each other on numerous occasions and had celebrated the end of the fighting. After returning home together those long years ago, they had determined to stay in touch, but life got in the way, and they did not communicate until Ted wrote his letter to Ralph. Ralph's wife, Judith, was so generous and loving that Sarah felt like she was being pulled into a family that she could relate to immediately. She had never before felt the kind of warmth that this good woman could produce so spontaneously.

She did not see her father during the daytime for the first week they were in Pittsburgh because Ralph was busy showing him around this wonderful industrial city and introducing him to men who were already in the Pittsburgh Iron Militia, the unit that he wanted Ted to join. Finally, on the Friday evening after they arrived, Ted and Sarah were sitting together in the front parlor, and Ted started to talk about his strong desire to join the militia there in Pittsburgh. "I will take you back to Knoxville before joining, or you could stay here with the Baxters and maybe even go to school with Minnie."

Sarah felt like her world was changing so fast that she wanted a chance to breathe before she decided. She had known of her father's desire to join the army, but she thought it would be the regular army, not some militia group that didn't even have proper weapons. She also hadn't even considered staying in Pittsburgh while her father was away. She felt her place was with Mary and the new baby back in Knoxville. But now she had a difficult decision to make because her new friends felt almost like family too.

The decision was made a little easier the next day when a letter came from Mary telling her of the new maid Herbert had bought who would also be a wet nurse for the baby, Dorothy. She let Sarah know that she had checked into a girl's boarding school for Sarah and would be pleased to enroll her when she came back. It didn't take long for Sarah to decide on at least a year of school with her new friend, Minnie. They would start together in March 1861. For Sarah, it was exciting—a new city, a new school, and a new friend. Minnie was overjoyed to have Sarah go to school with her. She wanted Sarah to meet her friends and felt like she now had a sister.

During the winter and early spring of 1861, Ted worked with Ralph Baxter during the day, and on most evenings and weekends, they drilled with the Pittsburgh militia brigade. Sarah was more than busy with her studies. It was the first time in her life that she was able to go to school full time, and she thrived in the classroom.

Finally, a few weeks after the change of national administration, the South made the biggest mistake of the century by opening a cannonade on Fort Sumter in South Carolina. President Lincoln called for seventy-five thousand volunteers to put down the rebellion. Sarah thought that calling out this many men was heavy-handed, but Ted explained to her that many in the North just wanted to make a large show of force that would bring the people of the South back to their senses and return them to the Union.

Before the beginning of May, the Pittsburgh militia marched off to the east to join other volunteer units that had responded immediately to the president's call. The war did not start with the planned quick military victory because neither the North nor the South was prepared with a large standing army. It started with bluff and blunders from both sides, and for the first month or two, there was more fear of the unknown than anything else.

CHAPTER 9
SARAH'S NEW FAMILY

Sarah was more than happy while living in Pittsburgh with Mrs. Baxter, Ralph, and Minnie. She was starting to make friends at school and found out how much she enjoyed science, math, and reading. She would not likely ever be as interested in history or writing or elocution or how to entertain in a formal way. She was able to do the required work for these classes, but in her favorite classes, she did more than what was required.

Late in the summer of 1862, when Sarah had been in school for more than a year, she received a letter from her father telling her that Mary was again expecting a baby and that her maid had run away. Herbert had not yet been able to buy another girl and was too cheap to pay a decent wage to anyone to help in the house. "Would you consider going to Knoxville to help Mary?" her father had asked. She felt he had the right to ask and even direct that she go, but she was so reluctant to leave Pittsburgh. She had grown to love the Baxters, and now that Ralph Junior had also joined the army, she wanted to stay with Minnie and her mother.

She was so happy to hear from her father at this time because the Northern army had suffered a number of defeats at the hands of the Army of Northern Virginia, under the leadership of Robert E. Lee, who had suddenly emerged as the most audacious Southern commander. She, along with the Baxters, had been so worried that one or both of their men had been injured or killed during the fighting, especially since the conflict was producing record casualties during the summer of 1862.

In spite of her reluctant feelings, she agreed to go to Knoxville to try to help, but she asked her father for permission to leave if the situation made her uncomfortable. Ted had left her with more than enough money to travel, and when she tried to pay Mrs. Baxter for her board and room, she was quickly and definitively rebuffed with a kind but clear answer. "You have been a better sister to Minnie and a daughter to me, more than if you had been natural born into this family. I will not accept money from a member of my family because you have meant so much to us."

They had had the discussion numerous times, and Sarah knew it was futile to try to change Mrs. Baxter's mind so on her final day, just before leaving, she left a note in the cupboard for Mrs. Baxter along with two twenty-dollar gold pieces.

The note read: "I know that we have talked over and over about me not paying for room and board, so I am leaving instead two pieces of gold for you to buy something for yourself and Minnie. I could never repay your love and kindness and don't think the amount left would begin to cover any expenses. It is simply a gift of gratitude and love. I hope that we will see each other again soon and that all of our men will know of our love for them. Love, Sarah."

With that, Sarah left for Knoxville with a growing sense of foreboding. She was worried that she might never see Minnie, Ralph, or Mrs. Baxter again. The feeling did not get any better during the long, roundabout journey back to Knoxville. As she traveled farther south, she became more and more concerned that she should not have brought her mules. She did not go near any battlefields, but the papers she read talked about the vast numbers of horses and mules that were being killed in the battles. She realized that by bringing her mules into closer proximity to the fighting, they could be requisitioned by the Southern army once they were back in Tennessee. She knew that she would need to be careful not to show them off and to keep them in Herbert's barn as much as possible. She wasn't even sure that Herbert would not try to sell them without consulting her.

Because of the circuitous route she was forced to travel, the trip to Knoxville took two weeks. This was a week longer than it had taken when she and her father traveled from Knoxville to Pittsburgh before the war. It now made a difference whether or not a person was traveling using a military pass. Even trains traveled more slowly in the border states because the engineers never knew if a raiding cavalry unit had torn up tracks or burned bridges or had attacked a watering station along the line, especially in lower Kentucky or anywhere in Tennessee.

Another thing that Mrs. Baxter had instructed Sarah to do was not to tell anyone about the amount of money she was carrying. When she needed a hotel room or feed for her mules or food to eat, Mrs. Baxter advised Sarah to use greenbacks whenever possible. Mrs. Baxter was worried that if anyone knew that the girl had any gold it would, at the very least, endanger her. She also advised Sarah not to be overly friendly with any man, and no woman under the age of sixty. That sounded a bit unrealistic to Sarah, but the closer she got to war areas, she realized that there were desperate-looking people at all of the train stations.

CHAPTER 10
1861, KNOXVILLE, TENNESSEE

Because of her anxiety, the journey seemed much longer than it really was. When she finally arrived at Herbert and Mary's home, she was completely worn out. Mary was so happy to see her, and even Herbert seemed relieved when she finally knocked on their door.

Mary took one look at her and said, "I won't ask how your trip was. It shows in your tired eyes. It looks like you have been awake for most of the two weeks that you have been traveling." Even though it was still early in the afternoon, Mary insisted that Sarah have some hot milk and go straight upstairs to bed. When she awoke the next morning, it seemed like she had not even turned over during that long, restful sleep.

Sarah settled into a routine of helping Mary and avoiding Herbert as much as possible. The avoiding wasn't hard because Herbert was so busy at the bank. He was shorthanded. Three of his tellers and a clerk had left almost as soon as the first gun was fired on Fort Sumter. He was amazed because three of them went to side with the North and only one enlisted in the Southern army. It was an indication of the politics in northeastern Tennessee, where their economy was not dependent on large plantations.

Herbert had always owned six or seven slaves to work in the house and around the property. He considered himself more akin to the plantation owners in the Deep South in attitude and politics than to most of his neighbors in Knoxville. Because of this, he had assumed that the people who worked for him were of the same mind. He was never one to observe more than the most superficial parts of an individual's personality.

Sarah slowly became aware of the gulf that existed between Mary and her husband. Mary was as neutral as possible politically and spent most of her time involved with her own children and their education. Herbert was active politically, part of a small group that met at night and would strive to undermine any connection between Northern sympathizers in Knoxville and the North. They had been compiling a list of those they knew had outspoken sympathy for the North and were trying to isolate them from the rest of the community. One of the strong tactics that Herbert used was to make banking as hard as possible for people on the list.

Sarah was with her aunt and uncle through the holidays and the cold days of January 1863. She knew that the slaves Herbert owned were becoming restive ever since they had heard about the Emancipation Proclamation issued by President Lincoln on New Year's Day. She wondered if more of them would try to run away, just as the maid had done the previous year.

One day early in February, Sarah hitched up her mules to take them for exercise and to pick up a few things at the shops in Knoxville. She was just setting off back home when she was accosted by two men dressed as Confederate soldiers. "We have a requisition and orders to pick up all healthy mules for use with the army," one of the men said.

"Well, you can't take these mules. They won't work for anyone but me," Sarah replied.

"We have some teamsters who can make any mule or horse work. I am sure that they will be perfectly able to make yours pull what we need," said the other man.

Sarah pulled out her whip to encourage the men to back away and then said, "I won't let you take them. I have raised them since they were born."

At that moment, she heard a voice behind her. "You had better let the men take the mules. It will save a lot of trouble."

Sarah turned to see a familiar-looking young man dressed in an officer's uniform. "Don't I know you from somewhere? You look like someone I should know."

"I am Lieutenant Murphy," he said, "and yes, I do know you."

She now recognized the young man, despite the addition of a handsome blond beard. "Chauncey Murphy, would you please tell these men that I can keep my mules. They don't have any right to just take them from me. Then, after you have fixed that problem, you can come to dinner tonight with my aunt and uncle. I think that your father knows my Uncle Herbert," she said.

"Yes, he is the person who put us in contact with your father before the first hunt in Tennessee." Chauncey told his men to go look for other mules or horses and that he would take care of this situation personally.

CHAPTER 11

CHAUNCEY COMES TO DINNER

That evening, after Herbert and Mary had gotten over the surprise and discomfort of Sarah announcing that she had invited a man to dinner without asking them, they welcomed Chauncey as if they had made the invitation themselves. The situation was helped when Sarah reminded Herbert that he knew Chauncey's father and had done business with him before the war. She also pointed out that Chauncey was serving in the Confederate army. Then Herbert started to think about the benefit to his bank if it were associated again with a large bank in the North, no matter which side won the war.

The discussion around the dinner table was mainly about what was happening in the east, where the news was mostly good for the Southern armies. They had held their own against the North and in fact had inflicted a severe punishing defeat against the army under General Burnside at Fredericksburg. Chauncey had missed that fight because he had been sent to gather as many recruits as possible from

Kentucky and Tennessee. The victory had made it easier for him to get young men and boys to join, thinking that they would be part of an army that would be led by Robert E Lee and would continue to give the North the licking that they deserved.

This talk brought up the subject of Chauncey and why he had decided to fight with the South against his boyhood friends and other members of his mother's and father's families. He was very open about his irritation with the federal government stepping in to enforce its will against the traditional, constitutional rights of self-determination of people in the states. "There are many areas that states should be able to govern themselves. States build their own roads, license businesses, settle disputes between cities and counties, and enforce laws regarding crimes. I believe the last thing you would want is to have the federal government step in and tell you how to run your bank, Mr. Ewing. What do you think?"

Herbert was taken aback by the last statement because it was certainly something that he had never considered as a possibility. Even though there had been bank crises and money failure on many occasions since the beginning of the republic, he thought that bankers knew best how to solve those problems. He felt like every time the federal government got involved in banking, it just muddied the waters. The most he thought they had a responsibility to do was establish a national monetary standard. When the federal government got involved in banking, it always favored the big banks to the detriment of the smaller, local banks. Chauncey's father understood that because he owned a large bank, he would benefit from more government control.

"I think that I have the same opinion as your father, Chauncey, about whether to have the government looking over my shoulder as I conduct daily business. Has he talked to you about what it will mean to him if the South wins this war?"

"He has never talked to me about politics or business and he threatened to cut me off without a cent if I joined the Confederate army, but he relented when he saw how strongly I felt about my reasons. I think that now he is just hoping that I will survive."

"We all hope that our loved ones survive," Mary said, joining the conversation. "I have a much-loved brother who is off somewhere in the east with men from Pittsburgh. I worry about him constantly, as I am sure Sarah does. We all hope that the war will not go on much longer."

"My father and I disagree about the outcome of the war, but I think enough lives have been lost and ruined so that now it would make sense to me to allow the people in the states to vote to end the war," Sarah said.

"It would be nice if it were that simple," Herbert said.

"Many people on both sides have voted with their lives to continue the war," said Chauncey. "I don't think that we can simply or lightly override their votes using a paper ballot."

Sarah was now embarrassed for having spoken up and decided to listen until Chauncey brought up the subject of her mules. She felt too strongly about just having them taken from her without so much as a request or apology for the demand. "Don't you think that just trying to take my mules contradicts the things you have just talked about? Or does the Confederate government have the right to take a person's mules without her permission?"

Now it was Chauncey who was on the defensive, and he tried to excuse the events that led up to his coming to dinner. "The men who were trying to get away with your mules were not my men really. They have been assigned to me to help get more mules and horses while I recruit men for the Army of Northern Virginia. If your mules were not so well taken care of, they wouldn't have bothered you. For my own part, I am able to pay a bonus to any man who will sign up using either Yankee greenbacks or Confederate money. Up in Kentucky, they prefer Yankee money."

"How do you get Yankee money?" Sarah asked.

At this point, Chauncey became more careful about talking freely about how he spent the winter months in the North. The past winter, he used a scheme in which he signed up in the Union army as a substitute for wealthy young men, and they would pay him in gold or greenbacks. He would go to the camp, become ill, and desert from hospital. Then he would go to another large city and repeat the same behavior. Over the winter, he had accumulated three thousand dollars by doing this, which made it a lot easier to recruit young men in Kentucky and Tennessee. One hundred to two hundred Yankee dollars would buy a lot more in Tennessee than an equal amount of Confederate money anywhere. He wasn't able to find any man in Kentucky who would accept Confederate money.

This was a not-so-subtle indication of how the war was really going. Even though the Confederates had won some spectacular victories over the Union army in the east, in the west, the Confederacy controlled a lot less territory in the early winter of 1863 than they had started with in 1861.

As Chauncey thought carefully about how to answer Sarah's question, Herbert made the comment that it was time to talk of something other than the war.

Chauncey responded, "We really do need men, mules, and horses in Northern Virginia, and I was hoping that Sarah would consider selling hers."

"I don't want to sell these two, but there may be some left down on the farm that we could sell. But I wouldn't want to take Yankee money for them. Even though I have now lived with people in the North, I still don't agree with them coming here and forcing these states to stay in the Union. I believe now that they have proclaimed all slaves in the remaining Confederate states to be free, they will push the war harder than ever."

"Don't those mules already belong to my father?" Chauncey asked. "He is leasing the farm from your father, and the livestock are part of the lease."

"I have the paperwork for the lease in the bank and can clarify who has a right to what on the farm," Herbert said. "I can get it from the vault in the morning if you will still be in Knoxville, Chauncey?"

"I should be here for a few more days. Why don't I meet you at the bank in the morning?" Chauncey suggested.

With that, it became more cordial and the talk moved onto how the banking business was going and other, more social topics.

CHAPTER 12

HERBERT'S NATURE

The next day, Chauncey showed up at the bank and asked to see Herbert for a few minutes so he could look over the lease. He wanted to see if there were any credence to the proposition that, even though his father leased the farm, all of the farm animals still belonged to (and could be controlled by) Sarah and her father.

During that conversation, Herbert brought out Ted's will and showed it to Chauncey. Ted had left his will with Herbert before he left for Pittsburgh and the war. It left the farm and all assets, which were substantial, to Sarah, should she outlive her father. If Sarah did not survive her father, and there were no direct heirs, then Herbert's wife, Mary, and her heirs would be the beneficiaries.

"You made a proposal last evening. You said you thought that Sarah could be more useful in and around Richmond than she is here in Knoxville," Herbert said. "After you left, she talked to Mary and me about the possibility of moving there in order to serve in one of the hospitals. Do you think that she would be able to travel there safely?"

Chauncey observed that there was more to Herbert's question than he was saying openly. He realized that Herbert was very concerned about the will and was far more dangerously avaricious than any man he knew. He also realized that Sarah would indeed be a lot safer away from Knoxville than living in the same household with this man.

"What do you propose?" Chauncey asked.

"I believe that Mary and I could spare her if she really wanted to travel to Richmond. If you would take her with your recruits, then Mary would feel Sarah was traveling in safe company. From what you've told us, you will be traveling down to Chattanooga before you cross the mountains to the east. That would take you close to the farm in Cleveland, and maybe you could talk Sarah into selling you any available mules from the farm."

From this, Chauncey realized how much Herbert was counting on putting Sarah in harm's way. He could not believe that a man could stoop so low as to hope that a family member would die because it would benefit him. Again, he was struck by the thought that Sarah would be much better off anywhere except in near proximity to her uncle.

"Herbert, I would guarantee that if Sarah was with my recruits, she would be as safe, or even safer than if she were sitting in your parlor. I trust my men completely," he said.

With that, the conversation ended, and a bargain was struck. Herbert would have Sarah ready to go with Chauncey when he was ready to leave Knoxville in a couple of days.

CHAPTER 13

1863, CLEVELAND

It only took them a week to reach Cleveland and her home. She found that the farm had not been properly worked because her father's men were off with the army, and their wives could barely keep up with caring properly for their families. She asked Chauncey if his father had any intention of hiring someone to work the farm during the war. Chauncey was at a loss for a few moments, then responded, "I haven't heard from my father since the war began. He sent me down to work the farm in January 1861. He thought that your father's men would help me. It worked well until the shelling of Fort Sumter, but then I left for the army and didn't let my father know."

Sarah was incredulous at this admission and wondered how Chauncey ever thought that the farm would be OK without the supervision of an owner or his agent. She looked Chauncey straight in the eye and said, "You need to let your father know that someone is needed to work the farm, and he needs to make arrangements, or you will lose the lease and the money he has already paid."

"I believe it to be more an issue between your father and mine than it is between my father and me," he said.

Sarah could not believe his total disregard for a business arrangement that Chauncey's father had intended to benefit his son in so many ways. She decided that, before they left Cleveland, she would send a letter to Mary and ask her to try to get word to Ted about the apparent breaking of the lease.

Sarah realized that even though Chauncey was older than her, his lack of judgment in this would need to be corrected. She decided she would figure out a way to correct him for his own good.

After the confrontation, Chauncey decided that in the future, he would not be talking to Sarah about her farm or mules or anything else regarding business. He would leave the arrangements for purchasing the mules to Sergeant Burgess, who had been sent along on this recruiting expedition to acquire horses and mules—and partly to keep Chauncey on a short leash. The young man from Boston was not completely trusted by his Southern superiors.

The company remained in Cleveland for two days while Sergeant Burgess made arrangements to purchase mules from Sarah and obtain more provisions for the journey. They intended to move east across the mountains and then northward, through North Carolina and Virginia to Lee's army. This march would last another four to six weeks and would prepare the men for living and fighting together. The one thing that Chauncey did understand about working with other young men and boys was the necessity of working together and maintaining strong discipline.

After the company left Chattanooga, the first few days of travel were really hard for Sarah, the other women, and the younger men and boys in the company. Most had been on farms all of their lives and had never dealt with the issues of living close to so many other people with differing backgrounds. In addition to the other trying conditions, the weather that winter was very cold, and some of the higher passes were covered in deep snow. It was extremely slow going through those areas, as the heavy-laden wagons needed the help of all the extra mules and men to get them over the high passes.

None of the recruits were familiar with military discipline, and it definitely was not what they were expecting when they enlisted with Chauncey. Every morning before breaking camp, the recruits were drilled and taught in the sternest way the need for working together—and for always supporting the men of their unit. In the military, there was not room for them to fight alone. The only way that their weapons would work effectively was to mass their fire, and the only way they could do that was to load and fire in unison with the rest of their company.

Travel at this time of year was always a challenge, usually because of the late winter and early spring storms that turned the roads and trails into sticky mud that sucked at both the mules' and horses' hooves and the men's boots. The wagon wheels would also get stuck, and men would have to figure out ways to force the wagons forward and onto firmer ground. Needless to say, progress was very slow. No one ever seemed to have dry clothing, and all the travelers and soldiers were footsore and exhausted.

The other problem was that there were five women, including Sarah, along with the company. Even though these women were there for various reasons of their own, the men were drawn to them like bears to honey. Sarah was not comfortable with most of the attention, and she wondered why Chauncey did not notice her anxiety. She was still enthralled by the chance to travel with the army, even though these were green recruits, but she watched Chauncey with avid interest. After the confrontation about the farm, Sarah had a hard time talking to Chauncey. She felt a weakness in her position now because he was clearly in charge of everything in the column. Away from the farm, she lacked the confidence to confront him.

Sergeant Burgess admired Sarah because he recognized in her many qualities that had drawn him to his own wife. Even though the march was as hard for her as anyone, she remained cheerful and uncomplaining. He recognized her skill with her mules and noticed that they were matched better than any other team in the column.

The two mules, for example, worked better to free themselves from the mud than any of the other teams. He also observed that the mules from her farm were bred from better stock than the others the company had picked up along the way. He was also aware of Sarah's attraction to Chauncey and wondered where that would lead. Even though her attitude was apparent to him, he also saw in her a level-headedness that he hoped would keep her out of trouble.

One day when the column was struggling up through a pass in the Appalachian Mountains, Sergeant Burgess and Corporal Jensen were watching with interest as the men came to a campground that had been scouted by Chauncey the previous morning. Chauncey had camped overnight and waited for the men to catch up with him. Chauncey came up to them as they were watching the men struggle to clear the wheels of the wagons from the mud. Chauncey noticed that it was not only the mules that responded to Sarah's direction and encouragement, but also the men who were taking instruction from her.

"Maybe I should step in and remind the men who is in charge of this company," Chauncey said.

"Do you think they would work as hard for you as they do for her?" Corporal Jensen asked.

"They might not, but she would then understand who is in command," Sergeant Burgess said.

"What do you mean by that remark?" asked Chauncey.

"I think it's obvious that she would gladly follow your commands," Burgess replied.

Chauncey studied the two men for a moment while he thought about how to respond. "If you mean what I think you mean, it would be like matching a thoroughbred horse with a donkey." Then he rode off toward the camp, leaving them behind.

Jensen looked at Burgess and asked, "Are you also thinking that he may not understand which one is the ass?"

Burgess smiled and walked off.

CHAPTER 14
1863, RECRUITS ON THE TRAIL

When the company left Cleveland to enter the mountains, there were two recruits that would have surprised Sarah, had she known who they were. They had observed her in the mountains with her father and remembered her, but they did not make themselves known to her. The Taylor brothers, Clarence and Amos, had been recruited in Chattanooga, and their father had sent a recalcitrant slave girl with them. "See if you can sell her along the way," he had said to them. "If you do, you can keep any money that she brings."

Sarah was aware of the girl and thought that it was strange that the two brothers brought her along but did not seem to give her any responsibilities. She looked ragged and tired all of the time, and Sarah suspected that she was not eating properly or sleeping comfortably.

One day, after the company had been traveling for about ten days, the girl was walking slowly beside Sarah's wagon and asked if she might have a drink of water. She spoke with a clear accent that Sarah thought sounded much too refined for the girl to have come from the South. Sarah stopped her wagon and got down to fetch a cup from a side cupboard that was attached to the outside of the wagon.

"What is your name?" she asked as the girl drank.

The girl looked carefully at Sarah with both suspicion and a little fear. Finally, she said, "I am called Mattie."

"Mattie, you look completely done in. Would you ride along with me for a while?"

The look of fear left Mattie's eyes. "I would like that, but I am not sure if those two devils will allow it."

Sarah now noticed that the Taylor brothers had stopped a short distance ahead and were watching the two young women talking. Finally, Amos approached and said, "Our father said that we could sell that girl if there was anyone interested." He spoke directly to Sarah, as if Mattie were a dumb animal that had no understanding of what he was implying.

Sarah was embarrassed and completely taken by surprise. Even though she had expressed strong feelings in the past about Southern rights, she had never considered that she or her father would ever own another person. She was even more astonished that Amos would speak like this without considering the young woman's feelings on the subject. But she also saw an opportunity to alleviate the horrible situation that the young woman found herself in.

She looked at Mattie carefully as she said to Amos, "Let me have her come with me for a few days and help me. Then I will give you an answer."

Mattie now looked very surprised, and the suspicious look came back into her eyes.

Amos was just as shocked at the response because he had only made the offer to try to easily get the girl away from Sarah. But now he thought that he might be able to get rid of a troublesome slave and make friends with a very attractive young woman.

"Well, if you agree to pay the full price after the trial period, then you can keep and feed her until we reach the army in Northern Virginia."

Sarah was relieved that this had been so easy. She did not realize that the two young men would feel that they would also now have the right to eat at her wagon whenever they wanted.

"When we get to the army, I will need to write to my father for the money. How much do you want?"

Amos thought for a few minutes and said, "I think the going price for a prime young woman is around seven hundred and fifty dollars. We would be happy to have that in either gold coin or greenbacks. In Confederate money, we would take a thousand."

There it was again, the difference in value between the money of the North and South.

Sarah had no idea about the fairness of the price, but she would be willing to buy the young woman and free her immediately if she could. So she agreed to the terms and then said to Mattie again, "Please climb up and ride along with me in the wagon."

Mattie quietly climbed up in the wagon, thankful that she would be able to ride instead of walk. Sarah noticed for the first time that she was barefoot and thought that her feet must be quite cold, since the column had been traveling in cold mud and snow for most of the trip. As Mattie got settled, Sarah said, "Your feet must be awfully cold. I have some rags that you can clean them with and a warm fur that you can wrap them in."

The two young women did not talk for the rest of that day's journey. Both were caught in their own thoughts of the likely future that this day's bargaining would produce.

Finally, in the evening, as they were preparing a simple soup at a small fire, Sarah said, "Mattie, I must confess that I do not like slavery, and when I 'buy' you, it will be so that you can be free. I will help you get wherever you would like to go when you are free."

Now Mattie had an opportunity to speak for the first time about the bargain that had taken place earlier. "I resent the fact that anyone can buy and sell me. I don't understand why anyone would think that I can be owned. If you buy me, it will be the third time it has happened, and I promise I will be just as angry and upset as the first time."

Sarah had thought that Mattie would express some gratitude about the promise of freedom but realized that she already considered herself free, just under the control of slavery.

"I am sorry, Mattie, that you and I don't understand each other, but I thought what I did"—Sarah hesitated—"I thought it would be helpful. Please help me understand what to do."

"I'm not sure what I want," Mattie said. "I was not born in this place and don't understand why people own other people."

They passed the rest of the day without speaking about anything related to the offered sale.

The next morning, the two young women only knew that their circumstances had changed, that they were in a situation neither had anticipated just two short weeks before. Sarah was as troubled as she had ever been in her life about any problem. Mattie was still resentful and sullen and wanted to tell Sarah about her life but did not know how much she trusted her. She would wait to find out.

All of the men, on the other hand, were relieved because the morning brought into view a trail that went mostly downhill and looked to be somewhat drier than any trail they'd seen for the past week. What they didn't know was the surprise that Chauncey planned for them after they got out of the mountains. Meanwhile, Clarence Taylor had a completely different kind of surprise in mind for a member of their party, and it would begin with better-cooked food than he had enjoyed since leaving home.

It began that afternoon. Chauncey announced that they would not stop to camp in the evening. They would have a light evening meal and start a forced march that would not end until the following evening. "You men have progressed so much more quickly than I anticipated that I feel you are ready to face the kind of marching that you will endure when facing the enemy."

The night march was far more difficult than anyone had imagined. It was a moonlit night, and there was a cold wind blowing. During this march, Sarah became more aware of the difficulties she would be facing if she continued with the army. She was used to working long hours on the farm, but she had always had the option of resting or getting warm when she needed. Now with someone else making the decisions, she felt a sense of helplessness that was foreign to her. Even the mules seemed to sense more danger and became balky about midnight. It also became obvious to Chauncey that the men would not be able to go much past midnight so he had the sergeant ride ahead and look for a good place to stop for the rest of the night.

When the small company finally halted, it was two o'clock in the morning, and everyone was completely spent. Some of the men just wanted to drop in their tracks, but the sergeants knew that if they did, the night was cold enough that they could lose some men to exposure. So they insisted that the men gather firewood and light small fires in order to warm themselves.

The Taylor brothers showed their value now due to the experience they had from hunting and often being in open country for nights on end. They had a sense, even in the dark, of where to look for small branches that could be used to make the kind of fire that would take the chill off the men. They heated rocks and laid them under their bedding, close to their feet so that they would be warmer when they slept. They also made sure that they placed their socks by these rocks so they would be dry when they put them on in the morning. Chauncey and his sergeants had never seen these techniques before and were surprised that these two, who had been raised on a plantation, were able to care so well for themselves and others.

The men mistakenly thought that the next day they would have a chance to recover from the day and night of little or no rest. Chauncey knew that they would face far more strenuous marches than this if they became part of Stonewall Jackson's "foot cavalry," so he had them up early the next morning and back on their way north by seven o'clock. By the end of this second day of forced marching, they had covered twenty-two miles. Chauncey knew that they could be asked to do a lot more than this in the face of the enemy, but he was satisfied that they had at a least a taste of what a forced march could be.

By evening, Clarence Taylor had had enough of obeying someone like Chauncey. He resented the fact that Chauncey wore an officer's uniform and that he spoke with a funny Boston accent. He also was bitter that he had not been chosen to lead a squad of men and that no one listened to him and his complaining. He was exhausted and not thinking very clearly, even as he and his brother Amos prepared to bed down for the night. Amos had seen his brother like this before and was always frightened by his brother's bad judgment at such times. Clarence had often been in trouble and needed someone like their father to restrain his more thoughtless activities.

That night, as Sarah and Mattie were going to sleep under the wagon, Clarence crept quietly to the back of the wagon and gently started to pull on Sarah's ankle. He was careful not to move too much at a time and was as quiet as when he was tracking any animal he meant to have for dinner, and he did not disturb the sleeping girl. Very carefully, he started to move her bedclothes aside. He felt a blinding flash of pain as Mattie suddenly swung the heavy handle of Sarah's whip with as much force as she could muster and hit him squarely between the eyes. She struck a second time before he could move out of range of her angry blows. Clarence recovered himself quickly and ran to where his brother was sleeping and woke him. Before the men in the camp were fully awake, they had picked up what they could of their few possessions, taken Chauncey's horse, and were racing for home. They gained the time they needed to find a good hiding place before Chauncey could get organized and find out what the commotion was all about.

Sergeant Burgess and two of the recruits were sent after them. If they were caught, Chauncey wanted to make a good example of them by having them shot. Not only had they deserted, but they had made the mistake of stealing his horse and some ammunition that the men would need when they reached the Army of Northern Virginia. Fortunately, Clarence and Amos could not carry much powder riding double, and it was thought that the three men would soon overtake them and bring them back.

Sarah was so shaken and upset by what had just happened to her—and the thought that any man would try to molest her in her sleep. She thought about going to Chauncey to see if he would leave her in the next village or town so that she could find her own way home. But the more she thought about it, she realized that she would not feel any safer among complete strangers, so she decided to stay on and just be more careful and on her guard.

The next morning, Sarah was so grateful to Mattie for what she had done. She asked Mattie about what had wakened her in the night.

"I've had experience with being disturbed at night." That was all that Mattie would say.

Sarah determined that she would keep one of her mules close, and if anyone approached during the night, hopefully they would disturb the mule, which would then wake her. She also resolved that no one would ever be told about the gold coins she carried for an emergency. She had thought at one point that someone should know about the coins but now realized that she could not fully trust anyone.

When the company had traveled for two more days, Burgess and the two men who were with him returned to camp. They had covered more than fifty miles back and had not seen any trace of the brothers or the horse. Clarence and Amos had given them the slip by hiding close by on that first night, and then, instead of heading back to Tennessee, the brothers set out toward what they thought was Richmond. They had gone northeast instead of west toward their home. It was Clarence's intention to join another Southern army under different names. He hoped that they would find some rich plantation boys who would pay him and Amos as substitutes. That was the one strategy that Chauncey had taught them that made sense.

Chauncey exploded in anger and threatened to break Burgess back to a common soldier for not sticking to the search longer. He suggested that any one of the recruits would have done a better job tracking. This mistake would come back to haunt him in the near future when Burgess reported to his commanding officer all of the events that reflected on Chauncey's ability to lead men. The men in the company also observed the outburst, and Chauncey lost any supporters he might have had.

Because of this incident, there was a lot of sullenness during the rest of the journey north to Lee's army. Chauncey, lacking the maturity to own that he had been part of creating the bad feelings, seemed to barely stay engaged with the men whom he had worked so hard to recruit.

Sarah observed the change of attitude in the camp carefully and became even more cautious and reserved. She became resolved that no one in this company would become a close friend. She felt it was unfair the way Chauncey was being treated by the other men.

CHAPTER 15

1863, NORTH CAROLINA AND VIRGINIA

During the next weeks, Sarah and Mattie settled into a routine that afforded both of them a chance to slowly get to know each other. And both started to appreciate the casual thoughtfulness that accompanied good friendships.

One day, as they were traveling, Sarah said to Mattie, half in jest, "I know that there has been a runaway slave law that provides for the capture of slaves who leave their masters. I wonder if there should be a runaway master law. Would you like to have Amos and Chauncey captured and brought back for punishment?"

Sarah had expected Mattie to be amused, but the look on Mattie's face was horrified. "If you had ever seen the worst of the punishment at a bad plantation, you would not think lightly of punishing runaways. I have seen crippled men who were made that way as punishment."

"Mattie, I have wanted to ask you a question ever since the first time I talked to you. You speak better English than any person I know, and I can't understand how you picked it up."

"It's a very long story and one that I am not sure anyone wants to hear. My way of speaking comes from a British doctor who raised me from the time I was about five years old. My family was taken from our village in Africa and forced onto a ship. My brother and I were tied together, and my parents were chained to the ship. My mother, father, and brother died on the voyage. That ship smelled worse than any place you can imagine. The doctor on the ship took pity on me and saved my life. For that, I love him and hate him."

"You are so young, and I know the slave trade was outlawed before you could have been born. How did you end up here in America?"

"Doctor McFarland bought me from the ship's captain and took me to his home in Bermuda where he and his wife taught me to read and write. She cared for me, and I believe loved me because she did not have any children. She died when I was about ten, and the doctor became very sad. He took a job in Mississippi, and we moved here. He was hired by a big plantation owner to take care of his people, but the doctor was very sad and started to drink a lot of the home liquor from the plantation. I think he drank too much, or he drank some that was bad, and he died.

"How old were you when that happened?" Sarah could tell from the hesitation in the tale that Mattie was debating whether or not to continue. "This must be very hard for you, Mattie. Are you sure you want to tell me?" she asked.

"I don't think you can understand any more of how I feel unless I tell you. But even then, you won't feel what I do. Let's wait until to-night when the work is done."

However, the subject was not brought up again that day or even that night. Both young women seemed to feel that it would take a qui-eter time for Mattie to be able to continue because of the extremely tender memories that were starting to well up and come forth.

Finally, a few days later, the men knew that they were a short dis-tance from Fredericksburg, where the Army of Northern Virginia was encamped for the winter. Chauncey wanted to take them on one more long march but did not want the encumbrance of the wagons, extra animals, and women. He decided to take the men on a circular march that would return them to their current camp after being out for over twenty-four hours.

It was quiet in the camp the evening the men left on the march, and Sarah again brought up the subject of Mattie's life in America.

"Before Doctor McFarland died, he gave me a paper signed by him and the owner of the plantation saying that I was a free person of color. He told me that I must keep that paper safe and not lose it, but one day someone got into my room while I was helping in the kitchen and must have taken that paper."

Sarah became upset about what she was hearing because she could guess that the person was the owner of the plantation, and he would only have one motive for stealing the paper.

"A few nights later, in the middle of the night, he came into my room. He told me to be very quiet and then took me. He kept coming back two or three nights a week and then stopped. I don't know if his wife found out, or if he became tired of me, or if he guessed I might be with child."

Sarah was horrified at the turn in the story. Ted had not really ever said anything to her about relations between men and women and especially not the practice of slave owners using their female slaves in that way. She started to weep quietly with Mattie, and the two women took comfort in each other's arms for a few moments.

"The baby that was born was my life, and I thought he had been given to me because so much had been taken away. I was so happy for four years, and then the master became angry because I was starting to teach my little Angus his letters."

"Why did you name him Angus?"

"That was Doctor McFarland's first name, and I thought it would make him happy. But the master was so angry, and one day, when I came back from the kitchen, my Angus was gone. He had been sold. Then the master sold me to a different plantation."

Mattie could not go on and collapsed into a quiet sobbing that was the most heart-rending sound Sarah had ever heard. All she could think of doing at that point was to sit as close to Mattie as she could so she could hold her head to her shoulder and rock gently. Both young women were tired and soon fell asleep sitting by the small, comforting fire.

CHAPTER 16

1863, VIRGINIA

S arah and Mattie worked quietly the next day around the small camp, neither of them bringing up the tale that had been told the previous night. Sarah wondered how Mattie was still alive after all that had been done to her, and she started to realize what her father was trying to teach her about the depth of feeling in all families. But Mattie was right to say that she could not feel the same.

The men finally returned later that night, and the camp was again noisy with the bravado of young men who had tested themselves and thought they knew what war would be like.

When the recruits finally reached the army, which was wintering around Fredericksburg, Sarah was appalled at the condition of the Confederate veterans and the animals. The men looked more like stick soldiers—they were so thin from lack of adequate provisions. In fact, she found out that part of the army had been sent south to scour the country for food and fodder. The men themselves were so poorly turned out that it looked like they were wearing last year's rags. The only newer clothes were blue instead of gray. She found out the reason for this was that after the battle of Fredericksburg, the Confederates had stripped the Yankee dead of whatever clothing was useful. There were groups of men sharing a single overcoat. They would take turns wearing it, especially if one had to go on picket duty during the night or in very cold weather. One of the favorite taunts thrown at the Northern pickets by these men was to ask when they were coming over the Rappahannock River again so that the Southern men could get more good clothes.

The condition of the animals gave Sarah pause as well because her mules were still in fine condition, especially compared to anything the army had around Fredericksburg. She made it clear to anyone who asked that her mules could not be used to pull cannon or caisson.

One day, when Sarah had been with the army about a week, she was approached by a man she did not know as she was cooking at her fire. He asked her if she had any coffee or even tea. He was from England and was dressed much better than most of the soldiers.

"Who are you?" Sarah asked.

"My name is Terrance Hogue, and I am here because my major asked me to find out if you have coffee. I want the tea for myself," he answered.

"Well, you can tell your major that I have not seen real coffee or tea for at least two months, not since I left Knoxville."

"That's too bad because if you had either, my major promised that he would make sure that you would not need to worry about your mules being requisitioned for other duties."

Sarah felt an almost instant disliking for this little man, who looked more like a shopkeeper than a soldier. "Does your major think that he can either take my personal property or that I would donate it to him?" she asked.

"Oh no, don't be offended! I thought that it would help if I used that threat to get what I wanted. It sometimes works and other times not. You see, I am not on close terms with any major. I serve as an orderly in the medical tents, and I help with the sick and wounded after the battles. Since it has been almost three months since the last big battle, I am not as busy so I decided to find out if I could get some real tea. You see, I am from England, and it's been months since I've had any real tea."

"It seems odd that you are here all the way from England just to serve as an orderly. You remind me more of my uncle, who is a banker."

Terrance decided that he liked Sarah even though at the time he did not realize that the comparison to her uncle was not complimentary. "That's funny because my only association with banks hasn't been very good for them. In fact, years ago I was given the choice to leave England for Australia or join the army because I had robbed a bank. I joined the army, headed off to fight in the Crimea, and ended up wounded in a hospital there. I was lucky because it was one of the hospitals run not by the military, but by a volunteer by the name of Florence Nightingale. She insisted on keeping the diseased soldiers away from the wounded and keeping both as clean as possible. I survived when most of the men who were in military hospitals were dying from infections."

Suddenly, Sarah was more interested in what he had to say, and then she noticed that one of his legs looked strange. He recognized her look and raised his left pant leg enough to show the wooden leg. "It's not as bad as it looks. At least it doesn't get cold like the other one," he said.

She noticed then that the leg was fashioned so that there a small, carved foot was part of the whole. "Mattie, come here and see this Englishman. I think his talk and his leg may interest you," Sarah called out. Mattie came over and looked at Terrance. "This is my friend Mattie, and I think she would like to see that leg."

"Does the foot make it easier to walk, or is it there for decoration?" Mattie asked. "The only other men I have seen with missing legs have used crutches or just had a wooden stump to walk on."

"Oh, my leg is completely different. It not only has the small foot, but the upper attachment is specially carved with a small cup for the soft part of the flesh. At first, when it was new, I could only walk without crutches for a few minutes. But very gradually, the flesh became insensitive to the pressure and pain, and now I rarely need any other support and can walk great distances."

As Sarah got to know Terrance over the next few days, she became more at ease with him. She had been uncomfortable around most of the men since Clarence had tried to attack her.

She met another soldier the same week whom she also made friends with. Nathaniel showed up at her cooking fire one night and asked if she needed any help. He was small and very clever about adding wild onion and other roots to the food rations of the men to increase the bulk of a meal. One of the benefits Sarah noticed was that the men she was cooking for now became a little more energetic in scavenging for firewood and other things that would make their camp a little easier to tolerate.

Nathaniel told Sarah he had been with the army since the previous summer and had been through the battle of Fredericksburg where he had first come under serious fire. He had been a new replacement in Early's division of Stonewall Jackson's corps.

There was something very odd about Nathaniel that drew Sarah to him. She realized she felt about him much like she felt for Ralph Baxter, more like a sibling than a friend. She started to develop the same worry for his safety as she had for Ralph's.

"I notice that you seem to watch a handsome young lieutenant whenever he is around. Do you know him well?" Nathanial asked one day.

Sarah flushed when she realized that she had been observed so closely. "Well, he's the one who talked me into coming with the recruits from Tennessee. He told my aunt and uncle that he would make sure that I would be safe. I realize now that he promised more than he could deliver. Plus, he really isn't interested in keeping that promise."

At the time that this conversation was going on, Chauncey was riding his new horse east to Skinners Neck. Once there, he intended to turn north to Aquia Junction and then southwest to Falmouth in order to gather information about the Union buildup of troops and supplies. He was not authorized to do this, but he had heard his colonel talking to one of the generals about the need to know more about the Yankee intentions and movements. He was taking a great risk because he had taken on the guise of a lost traveler and could be taken for a spy if he were found out. He had one advantage that would help him if he was caught, and that was his heavy Bostonian accent. He certainly did not sound like he was from anywhere near the South.

Considering the number of Union troops in the area, the ride went well for the first two days. He was able to make friends with some of the troops along the way by asking for directions to Falmouth before riding on. Then, on the outskirts of Falmouth, he ran into trouble in the form of a Negro guard who pointed a rifle at his chest and demanded that he get down from his horse. Chauncey started to sweat nervously and realized that this man held not only the success of his spying, but also his life in his hands.

He decided to continue to act as he had the past two days and introduced himself to the man. "My name is Chauncey Murphy, and I am headed for Falmouth. What's your name?" he asked.

This seemed to catch the guard by surprise. He replied, "My name is George Washington Lee, and you are going to walk your horse over to that building. Then you will wait inside while I get my officer."

CHAPTER 17

1860, PHILIDELPHIA

George Washington Lee was the great-grandson of Billy Lee, who had been a favorite slave at Mount Vernon, the constant companion of George Washington during the Revolutionary War. He continued to serve George Washington when he was the president. Billy Lee later married a free Negro woman from Philadelphia who refused to live with him in Virginia because she did not want to risk becoming enslaved. She had a son, who would later become George Washington Lee's grandfather, and she established a good home in Philadelphia for her son.

Her son Benjamin and then his son Alexander had been cabinet-makers, so it was natural for George to follow their trade. Just a few years before the Civil War started, young George was apprenticed to a cabinetmaker in Philadelphia.

George's mother had not heard from her husband, Alexander, since he left to deliver some furniture to a customer in Baltimore in May of 1857. There was always danger for a free Negro man travel-ing to a slave state because he could be accused so easily of being a runaway slave, but George's father had two letters with him, one from the cabinet maker and another from his Quaker friend, both identifying him as a free man from Philadelphia. With these, he thought he would be able to travel to and from Baltimore safely. All that was known about his disappearance was that he had made the delivery as he normally did. From that point on, no one had heard from him.

George was apprenticed to the cabinet shop that same year and had shown so much talent that by May of 1860, he was ready to become a qualified cabinetmaker working for real wages.

One day in late May 1860, George Washington Lee's morning started like any other, but an event took place that should have been insignificant, but it was an event that for him had profound consequences. He was walking to work in Philadelphia when he spotted a large, ornate carriage. It was black with red-and-gold trim and floral decorations. It was pulled by four perfectly matched black horses and attended by the smallest coachman George had ever seen. George thought at first that he couldn't be more than twelve years old. As he approached in a friendly mood, he said, "Good morning, my little man."

His mistake was in the tone of his voice and his demeanor. The small Negro turned toward him and spit on the walk in front of George's path. George flushed with anger at the affront. "What do you think you're doing?" As the man turned to face him, George realized that he was much older than George had thought, and he was angry.

He said to George, "I guess you think because you're a free nigger and bigger than me that you are somehow better."

"How do you know I'm free?" George asked.

"Because of the way you strut and talk."

"Well, I am free, but that ain't no reason for you to spit in front of me."

"Why did you call me 'little man'?"

"I meant no disrespect. I thought you were a young boy."

"I been a slave for thirty years, and do you know something? I will be until I die lest someone helps me. But you ain't much freer than me. You have a white world all around you, and no matter how hard you try, you can't get into it. Just like being locked up behind a high white fence."

With that, the coachman turned his back on George and went back to shining the carriage.

George continued on his way to the cabinet shop where he had been working for three years, and where he had found the closest thing to acceptance in his predominately white world. He wanted to talk to Mister Jeff about what the coachman had said to him, but he didn't find a good time until toward the end of the day.

"How many people avoid you, and how many toughs spit at you on your way here every day?" Jeff asked.

As George thought about this, he realized that he had stopped noticing the number of people who mistreated him as he walked the streets of Philadelphia. It was too true that in his life, there was a world within a world. He knew he couldn't change it, and so now it started to bother him. He had a brief moment of wondering what it would be like to be able to move freely in the other world. He also started to wonder what it was like for that small black man to be trapped in his world, which must be far more confined than his.

The only reason he was free, he knew, was because of his birth. His great-grandfather had been emancipated by George Washington, and his great-grandmother was born free. Emancipation didn't mean as much at the moment. He knew he could not travel safely on his own. He had heard of men who had been taken from the streets of cities and sold into slavery even though they were born free. He was sure that this was the reason for his father's disappearance.

As he was thinking about this, a familiar carriage pulled up in front of the cabinet shop. George recognized the small coachman on the driver's platform, and next to him was another footman in livery. The footman jumped down and opened the door for the owner, who got out and looked around, as if trying to locate a business. He turned toward the shop where George was looking out the window and immediately recognized what he wanted. He took the few short steps to enter the building and nodded to Jeff, who said that he would be with the man right away.

George had a hard time taking his eyes from the very well-dressed black man. He listened carefully as the man explained to Jeff that he wanted a fine dining table with chairs, a sideboard, wine cupboard, and buffet. George realized that the man was placing a large order for himself, not for a master. As these thoughts dawned on him, the implications astonished and confused him. He had heard that there were black men who owned slaves, but he had never been confronted by the reality—especially a man who was dressed so fine and who rode in one of the richest-looking carriages he had ever seen.

When the order was placed and understood, the man turned and walked out, apparently not noticing George any more than any other customer of equal rank or wealth. When he regained his composure, George noticed Jeff looking at him with a knowing look. "You look like you need to have about a year to think about what you have just seen."

"I heard that in the South, there are Negro men who own other Negroes, but I never thought I would see one," George answered.

"It's rare to see any slave owner brave enough to venture this far north, but this man does business here in Philadelphia every few years, and any tradesman remembers him. This is the second time he has ordered the same kind of dining-room furniture from me."

"I don't understand how he can look so rich."

"Well, he is rich, and I believe he wants to show anyone who is interested that he is not only a free Negro man but one of substance," Jeff answered.

When the conversation ended, George went back to work on a chair back. One day, he hoped to be as good as his fellow worker, old Moses, at carving fancy figures on the decorative parts of furniture.

Now he could do basic patterns and was more than competent in building strong tables and chairs and cabinets.

He was preoccupied, troubled with his own thoughts, the rest of the day and did not realize that it was time to go home until Jeff tapped him on the shoulder and pointed to the door.

When he reached home, he talked to his mother about the conflict with the small carriage driver and the shock of seeing the rich Negro planter. He looked around their small, three-room home where the family of five lived, and he realized for the first time that he could be rich like the planter. He thought that his mother deserved a lot more from life than the small home and meager living she was able to make from sewing and mending clothes. With that and the small wage he earned, they were able to keep their family together, but there was no extra money to buy luxuries of any kind.

George knew from the news and talk at the cabinet shop that the Republicans had a chance to win the election in the fall, and that a man named Abraham Lincoln might be the new president. There was more talk that the people in the South were considering leaving the Union if that happened. Some even said that if that happened, there would be a war between the states. Like any young man, George had no idea what war was really about, but he thought that he would want to be in on the fighting.

"Mama, if it comes to war, would you let me fight?" he asked.

Alice looked at him, for the first time aware that her son might fight and possibly die in a war. She knew in reality that he was old enough to make that decision on his own without any permission required from her, but she said, "Your great-grandfather was in the war with George Washington, and even though he faced the same danger, he didn't do any fighting. He was a slave and took care of the general, but he said that there were a lot of free black men fighting in that war, and if they had asked him to fight, he would have. Do you really think you would want to fight?"

"When I was walking down the street today and met that small black man, he made it clear that if he was a slave, then I was not free. I think that I would want to fight for his freedom and mine. His master was a rich black planter from Georgia."

Alice said that she had heard of black slaveholders but thought it was just a lie told by the white planters to partly justify their own use of slaves. "Black or white, slavery is wrong. There is no way that one person should own another and take the labor of that person's hands for his own use." She made it clear to George that if he truly wanted to join in the fight, she would bless him for it.

CHAPTER 18

1863, VIRGINIA

George had been with the Union army since the first year of the war. At first, he was a kitchen helper, but a couple of months ago, he had been given a musket and made a paid guard.

George was not sure if he had done the right thing in putting the arrogant man in the guard shack while he looked for someone to question him. He did know that he would not leave the man's horse where he could easily come out of the shack and ride away. It seemed to him that because the man had a Northern accent, he did not really need to worry too much about his escaping, but he wouldn't take any chances.

When George found Lieutenant Short, they both went to the shack and found that Chauncey had gone missing. No one around seemed to know who they were talking about.

"It's a good thing that you had that horse, or I would have thought you were seeing ghosts," Lieutenant Short said.

"It looks like a good horse. I wonder why he would just leave without it?" George said.

"I don't know for sure, but we believe there have been about three or four spies through here every week, trying to see what we are doing. We like to capture some of them just to send them back with bad information," said the lieutenant.

"Is there any real information we could give them that they can't see for themselves?"

"Just the timing and direction of the next attack. Since we don't know what's on Hooker's mind, all we can do is mislead them. We have caught a few and released them because we could not prove that they were spies, so each went his way with a different tale to tell. We hope it helps a little."

"Sir, I have been wondering when it would be my turn to be sent to a regular fighting outfit?"

"You've been with us almost since the beginning, working first in the kitchens, and then we put a gun in your hands and made you a guard. There will be plenty of chances for you to get into the fighting, but the captain wants to see if you can be made a junior officer or, at the very least, a noncommissioned officer. There will be opportunities for you to lead men of your own race, and I dare say that you will do it much better than any of us."

"I can't lead or follow anyone from here," George said. "By the way, what are we going to do with his horse? Looks like he would be a real good animal if someone were to take good care of him."

"Yes, he does look like a horse that some high-ranking officer would love to have shot from under him." Then Lieutenant Short thought to himself that maybe he could offer the horse to someone who could help both him and George get what they wanted. "George, I think we can use that horse to get you to a real unit. How would you like to be in the cavalry?"

"Let me learn to ride. Then maybe a cavalry assignment would be good."

George thought that this horse was looking better all the time. What he didn't realize was that most of the Union cavalry recruits didn't know how to ride before they signed up. They learned to ride after they were assigned to a unit. He also didn't understand that the recruits didn't own their own mounts. The horses were all furnished by the army.

During the next several weeks, he spent every spare moment learning to ride. If he had the opportunity to join a cavalry troop, he wanted to be ready.

CHAPTER 19

1863, FALMOUTH, VIRGINIA

C hauncey walked out of the guard shack as soon as he noticed that no one was really paying any attention to him. As he started to walk toward Falmouth, he was offered a ride by a Negro teamster who thought that he looked a little tired and upset.

Chauncey was happy to accept the ride but very quickly tired of listening to the man's conversation, partly because he was so upset at having been accosted by that nigger guard. In fact, Chauncey was so angry during the short trip that he heard only one small bit of information, even though the black man talked nonstop the entire way, without apparently needing to catch his breath. He was able to confirm that "Fighting Joe Hooker" intended to begin the spring offensive as soon as possible with the army encamped across the river from Fredericksburg where they had suffered one of the most lopsided defeats in the war. Chauncey wondered where that next big attack would start.

What really filled his mind, more than the conversation of the teamster, was a slow-building, angry burn that he had lost his horse and, on top of that, to a nigger guard who would certainly sell or give the animal to someone who did not know its value. There were times during the ride that he could feel himself flush with anger as he pictured the rifle pointed insolently at his chest. He hoped that he would have a chance to see the man again so that he could humiliate him. He imagined a variety of ways that he could punish George Washington Lee for what he had done.

Soon enough, he was at the village. He jumped down from the wagon without a word of thanks or acknowledgement to the man who had given him the ride. He then went to find a livery stable that could sell or rent him a horse to get back to Fredericksburg. He found a man named Abe Silver who specialized in picking up used-up horses from the cavalry and rehabilitating them before reselling them to the US government. Much more important to Chauncey was the fact that Abe Silver was a hidden Southern sympathizer who passed the news to Chauncey that the army had been buying horses, and that it looked like a move would take place very soon.

Abe sold Chauncey a good horse in exchange for a draft on his father's bank for double its value. He gave Chauncey directions that would take him safely back to Skinners Neck, where he could ford the river and return quickly to his unit. He then left Falmouth, trying not to draw attention to himself so that there would be no delays getting back across the river. Now in his mind, he was already formulating the report he would give. He would not be able to give totally accurate information, but by embellishing what he had seen and heard, he would let his commander know that the Yankees were definitely preparing for another big push across the Rappahannock River. He could see that just from the amount of activity going toward Falmouth and from the information Abe had given him.

He was so absorbed about the report and events of the last three days that he missed the trail to Skinners Neck and was lost for a time along the river. He was lucky to find a small tavern where he stayed the night. In the morning, he asked for directions back to the river crossing.

CHAPTER 20

1863, MARION

When Sarah arrived, she was sent to an area near Fredericksburg to help with the needs of some of the men who had spent a hard winter just trying to survive after the December battle. She quickly made herself useful by cooking and, more importantly, by mending clothing that would have been thrown away or turned into rags back home. The recruits she had arrived with were taunted because of the relatively new condition of their clothes. Some of them were so self-conscious about their appearance that they unwisely traded bits and pieces of their extra clothing for items of little or no value. They were often talked out of a good pair of socks or a warm scarf or gloves by cagey veterans who would give them a scavenged piece of equipment taken from a Yankee soldier who "didn't have any more use of it."

The more she became acquainted with Nathaniel Baker, the more she wanted to know about this boy from Georgia who had her mending clothes for him. Nathaniel had told her he came from a family of nine girls and only one other brother. He was right in the middle so had been pampered by older sisters and teased by the younger ones. The family did not have much money, but being farmers, they had enough to eat and could manage to scrape by most years. When Nathaniel signed up for the army, he gave his family most of the substitute's bounty he had received from the son of a wealthy plantation owner.

One day, as Nathaniel was watching Sarah prepare some skinny chickens for the pot of soup she was making for the men, out of the blue, he said, "Nathaniel isn't my real name."

Sarah looked up in surprise. "What?"

He repeated, "My name isn't really Nathaniel."

"Well then, what is it?" she asked.

He looked around carefully to make sure that no one was within earshot. "Promise you won't tell anyone." He paused and then said, "I'm really a woman, and my name isn't Nathaniel. It's Marion."

Sarah was so surprised that all she could do was stare dumbly and listen.

"I was born soon after my oldest sister, Mary, died, and I was named after her. I signed up with my fiancé, Edmond Nelson, and we came north from Georgia about a year ago. We were with the army when there was fighting close to Richmond. Then we came here and were in the fight around Fredericksburg. We were assigned a place behind a long stone wall. We were so safe there that we thought nothing could harm us, but then a lucky shot hit Edmond while he was talking to me. The light went from his eyes in midsentence. Nothing could have hurt me more than his death. I wanted to lie down and die right beside him. Before that battle, we left on a short, unauthorized furlough and were married. The minister wanted me to turn myself into our company commander to be sent home, but I refused and begged him not to tell anyone about us. I had him enter my name on the certificate as Marion because I didn't want my sister's exact name. The only comfort I have had since Edmond's death is that we were married first."

Sarah could hardly understand what she had just been told. She took a good long look at Marion. She had heard rumors that there were some women who dressed as men and then enlisted in both armies, but they were thought to be so few in number that she couldn't imagine really meeting one of them. Her thoughts as she looked at Marion came so quickly that she was confused. She thought Marion looked more like a young girl than a woman. She also thought that Marion looked like the marriage had been a necessity. If that were true, Marion should leave for home immediately.

"How can you stand staying here then?"

"This is something we were doing together, and we both felt strongly about it. I haven't changed in that way, and besides, what would I go home to?"

"I don't know, but it seems like it would be so lonely for you here. I heard that there were some women who were fighting with their men, disguised as men. Does anyone else know who you are?"

"I haven't told anyone, and I don't think anyone suspects. I heard of another woman that was fighting, and everyone found out when she was wounded. Even though she recovered, they sent her back home and told her not to come back."

Then Sarah said, "I guess they think we are good enough to cook, wash their clothes, and nurse them when they are sick or wounded, but we shouldn't be allowed to fight beside them." Sarah sighed, knowing this to be the truth but not liking it. "So your name is Marion Nelson?" she asked. "Why have you told me this now?"

"Because I need someone to know who I am in case I am killed, someone who can let my family know what has happened to me. I wrote a letter to Edmond's family and hope that they will not tell anyone who and where I really am."

"How old are you?"

"I joined when I was sixteen, and now I am seventeen."

Sarah looked again at her closely and thought that she didn't even look sixteen, let alone seventeen. "What am I going to call you? All of a sudden you don't look anything like a Nathaniel."

"I know. It's hard for me to feel anything like Marion or Nathaniel. Even though I want people to believe I am a man, I don't feel like one inside. I worry that I am going to give myself away."

Then Sarah asked a question that she had long wanted to ask someone who had been in the fighting. "Are you afraid during the battles?"

"I am when we are marching to the fight, but once it starts, I don't think much about being hurt or dying. I just fight."

Sarah wanted to know so much more, but she held herself back. "How long do you think it will be before the Yankees will give up and go home?"

"I don't think they will ever give up. The way they kept coming after us at Fredericksburg, you would think that they were not worried about dying or being hurt. Even though we continued to kill and wound them, they just kept coming. We were close to many of them and could see the determination on their faces. If they ever have officers that know what they are doing and realize that we are just like them, you will see the end of the war and no separate country."

This last thought worried Sarah for her father. She had not heard from him since before she left with Chauncey, and now she wondered if he were still unharmed or even alive. She had been aware, in the back of her mind, of the possibility that he could be hurt or killed, but she always hoped that he would somehow be spared. She worried that he might be with an officer who was fearful and hesitant or clumsy. She really couldn't talk to very many people about her fears because he was fighting in the Union army. But now she felt she could confide in Marion the same way she had confided in her.

"I worry about my father. He's in the Union army. I haven't heard from him since before Christmas last year."

"Do you know where he is?"

"He's never really said, only that he is just north of the Rebel army that they are trying to keep out of Washington. I guess that means that he was at Fredericksburg."

"So many have been killed or wounded, but more survive by far. It really depends on luck, I believe. Almost as many die from disease and sickness as in battle. The long winter months of boredom and exposure to the cold and bad food are sometimes our worst enemy," Marion said.

Sarah thought about this last comment and realized that her picture of what her father had been doing for the last two years was completely false. She thought that he had been constantly in battle against the gray-clad Southern armies. She had also pictured that the two armies were full of men who were in the best of condition physically and emotionally. Quite a different reality had presented itself when she first arrived in the camp of this great Southern army. Along with the less-than-well-dressed soldiers, she had witnessed how they were malnourished and, in most cases, ill-equipped for the cold camp. She also found out that in some cases, there were quite friendly relations between the opposing armies wherever there was close contact between the guards and pickets who faced each other across the Rappahannock River. She heard that each would taunt the other side with graphic humor. They also shared news and other items of value that made the contact somewhat compromising as far as knowledge about corps or division locations.

As Marion said her good-byes, Sarah started to wonder idly where Chauncey had gotten himself to. It had been several days since she had seen him, and she realized that he had disappeared without a word.

The next morning, the twenty-eighth of April, he suddenly appeared at her wagon asking if she had anything like hot coffee.

"The closest thing I have is a hot drink made of hominy and scorched wheat kernels. The men seem to tolerate it, probably because they don't have to fix it."

"Is it hot?"

"It's in the kettle hanging by the fire. It should be plenty hot."

When Sarah asked him where his horse was, he knew he shouldn't tell her, but he could not resist the temptation to let her know he had been up among the Yankees.

"I lost him to a nigger guard up just outside of Falmouth," he said. With that statement, he glanced at Mattie and asked, "Is she still with you? I thought she would have run away by now."

Sarah was irritated by this last comment and stiffly said, "Yes, my friend Mattie is here, and I hope that she will stay as long as she feels welcome with me. What in the world were you doing over there behind the Union lines?" The last question was asked with more than a little sarcasm in her voice.

Chauncey again realized he should not have told her where he had been, but Sarah was only a young woman so he didn't feel too threatened. He figured she would never tell anyone about his whereabouts.

"I wanted to see if they were getting ready to move down the Potomac," he said.

"Could you tell what they were up to?"

"All of the movement of supplies was from Aquia Landing toward Falmouth, so it looks like any attack will be close by."

"Who will you tell?"

"I'll tell my colonel." With that, he seemed to remember that he should be about his duty, and he left abruptly.

Sarah was still left to wonder if her father might be just across the river, and that gave her some comfort, as well as concern.

CHAPTER 21

1863, CHANCELLORSVILLE

The Union movement that began the next day caught the Confederate army by surprise. It began upriver from Fredericksburg at a sparsely defended ford across the Rappahannock River. For the first day, it seemed that the blue-coated army could move just where they wanted to, but then their "fighting general" changed from thinking about pursuing the Rebels to hunkering down and going into a defensive posture.

Sarah only learned bits and pieces about the battle as wounded men were brought to the medical station where she was helping. From the first day of the week-long battle, it was confusion and noise and turmoil. She was helping Terrance as much as she could, and during their few quiet moments, they visited more about his experiences in the Crimea. He was especially fond of talking about his time in the hospital run by Florence Nightingale, where he learned a great deal about the care of wounded and sick that would save lives.

He again tried to teach Sarah more about how to keep the men as clean as possible and use whatever came to hand to accomplish that.

She learned from him that clean water mixed with some strong spirits could be used to clean a wound and would help most men heal faster.

She observed that most doctors in the camps didn't think much of Terrance's methods, and there seemed to be an institutional resistance to any change that would require a higher standard of cleanliness. Most of the doctors were older men who were convinced that medicine had done all that it was able to do and that the rest of any healing was in the hands of God.

Sarah was so exhausted by the end of the week-long battle that she could hardly remember any particular day. It seemed to have been one long, continuous day, punctuated only by periods of brief rest. Some of the conversations with the dying men were so poignant that she thought she would remember them for the rest of her life, but at the end of the week, she could not recall anything except the raw emotion of trying to save a life and then watching the person die. She wondered for days afterward what this killing was all about. It seemed to make little sense when the week was over, and the Union army had retreated back to Falmouth, and the Confederate army reoccupied their positions around Fredericksburg. Not knowing what was in the minds of either government or the military leaders, all she had to go on were the rumors that circulated daily through camp.

There was plenty of recrimination, both conversational and official, from the Northern camp about why an army with superior numbers, endless equipment, and supplies could not subdue the Rebels, who were approximately half their number and poorly supplied. Perhaps Abe Lincoln said it best when he advised General Hooker before the battle to put in all his men. General Hooker, for whatever reason, never fought with more than one fourth to one third of his available men in any single battle of the long Chancellorsville campaign.

When Marion came back to the camp after being gone with Jackson's men, she still maintained that the South could not ultimately win the war against an enemy who seemed to have unlimited men and resources. "When they get leaders who know what they are doing and are not afraid of us, they will start to win the battles and the war," she repeated.

When Sarah saw Marion again, she looked at her friend for a few moments before saying, "I think that your war should be over now. You may think that you can hide that you are a woman, but pretty soon even the men will know that you are going to have a baby."

"Am I showing that much?" she asked.

"I can tell now because I'm looking closely, but in a few weeks, even the single men will know," Sarah answered. "Then the jig will surely be up."

"Would you go with me to talk to the lieutenant? He seems to be so rough that I am afraid of what he will either do or say."

"Yes, I believe I saw him a while ago over by his tent, and I think that now is the best time to tell him. You might as well get it over with and then leave camp and head for home."

Marion was reluctant to talk about returning home. She was afraid that, with her family circumstances being what they were, she would just be an added burden on their limited resources. She had not spoken to Sarah about her idea that maybe she could stay around Richmond and find work to support herself.

To say that the lieutenant was surprised when Nathaniel told him that her real name was Marion and that she would soon have a baby would be a cruel understatement. The lieutenant had come from a long line of men who felt that women should be dominated and kept in their place. The fact that Marion had performed as well as any soldier during the attack Stonewall Jackson's men made from the wilderness was borne out by his own observation of her conduct during the battle. She had not shown any signs of fatigue on the long march and had not shrunk from the fighting once the shooting had started. It was doubly amazing because those troops of Stonewall Jackson were known to be valorous beyond any others in the Confederacy. He told her that she would be excused from duty until he spoke to the colonel about her situation. He thought that there might be an example made of her to discourage other presumptuous females from thinking that they could fight in the army.

Sarah was surprised at his attitude and didn't hesitate to let him know that she thought that he could treat Marion with a lot more humanity. "Let her come with me and help in the camp today. I am sure that by tomorrow, she will be on her way home, and I would like to see that she makes a good start."

"Can I trust you to keep her here until tomorrow?" he asked sarcastically.

The next day, Colonel Shirtz was amazed at the story that Lieutenant Stevens told him, first about Marion having disguised herself as a man, and second about her exemplary service during the battle. He was even more surprised than Stevens that she was able to fight alongside her husband and then, when he was killed, to stay with the army. He said, "Why do you think she didn't come forward after Fredericksburg?"

"I don't think she would have come today except that Sarah Clarke insisted because she knew that the girl was pregnant."

Colonel Shirtz was then completely astounded at two facts: one, that the young woman was able while pregnant to go through a battle without being an impediment to those around her, and two, that Stevens wanted to have her disciplined as an example to the men. He said "Listen carefully to me, Lieutenant. It will never be my policy to reward valor with anything but praise. She may have broken every social law that I know of, but I am only concerned with her actions while on the march and in battle. Please take me to see her now."

When the two men arrived at the wagon where Sarah was with Marion, they found the two women not talking to each other, and there was an obvious air of hostility.

Colonel Shirtz asked, "What's the matter here?"

Marion said, "I don't want to go home. My husband is dead, and I worry about what my family will think of me. Sarah thinks that I would be much better off leaving than staying. Why can't I stay and serve in the hospital, or help Sarah for a while?"

Colonel Shirtz thought for a few moments and then responded, "You can better serve your husband's memory by having his child and raising that child to be a credit to its father. Your husband and you have given more than a full measure of valor and blood to the cause. I am sure that your parents will want to see and help raise their grandchild, and that means not only your parents, but also your husband's parents." He then took a Yankee ten-dollar gold piece from his pocket and placed it gently in her hand. "If this army gave medals like other armies do, you and your husband would both receive one for going far beyond your duty. Please take this. It should be enough to get you home."

With that, Marion finally broke down and started to weep. She was clearly touched by the colonel's thoughtfulness, and beyond that, she was confused and exhausted. "I don't know how to thank you, Colonel. I never expected this kind of compassion."

"One more thing, Marion. Please don't encourage any sisters or female friends to try to find husbands in the army. It would be too distracting for the men, and there are more like Lieutenant Stevens here than you would want to know," Colonel Shirtz finished.

Sarah had observed the colonel's kindness and then saw the twinkle in his eye when he said this last thing. In response, she said, "I don't know, Colonel, I think Stevens just likes to talk tough around women because he is so afraid of them. He would probably like to find a wife who will do everything that he says."

Stevens's face turned purple as he mumbled something. Then he turned on his heel and left this gathering that he did not understand and did not want anything more to do with.

CHAPTER 22

1863, CONFEDERATE MOVE TO PENNSYLVANIA

After the fighting around Chancellorsville, Lee rested his army for a short time and then started to move north. He wanted to take the fight into Maryland or Pennsylvania so that Northern Virginia would be spared the fighting for at least a season. He also hoped that the Northern people would become tired of fighting a foe that would not give up. If that were the case, then a truce could be engineered and a peace negotiated with a good possibility of two separate countries being formed. What he worried about was the war in the west, where the North now controlled most of the states of Louisiana and Tennessee along with most of the Mississippi River. He was hoping that a strong push north by him would cause panic and force General Grant, whose men were campaigning against Vicksburg, to send some troops east to help protect Washington.

No one could foresee how his move would truly affect the outcome of the war, but his effort in the summer of 1863 was designed to do as much damage as possible to the morale of the people of the Northern states.

Sarah and Mattie were following in the tail end of Jubal Early's Corps, which was part of one of the three great armies headed north across western Maryland. She was completely amazed at the size of this army and how much dust they could generate in the miles-long column. She was sure that the road would be marked for a hundred years simply from the number of men and beasts and wagons that were passing along its rutted length. At the end of each day, the men and animals were covered with dust to the point that even their teeth were caked with dust and some were hard of hearing because of the amount of dirt that had collected in their ears. The two young women learned early on to cover their faces with thin scarves to help keep off the dust and grit. The most anyone saw of them during the day were small openings in the cloths that showed their eyes.

Even though the movement into Northern territory was an adventure for Sarah, she sensed that the farther the army traveled, the tenser the men were becoming. Some were starting to grumble because they had not yet seen any serious enemy scouting. Others were afraid that the whole army would be trapped up north and kept from returning south until the end of the war. Even if only one of the columns were cut off, it would prove disastrous for the entire army.

If the men had known that Lee had lost all contact with his main cavalry, then they might have become even more panicky. They had passed through western Maryland and were now on the border of Pennsylvania. If they entered that state without the eyes of the cavalry, then there could be serious consequences.

As they were getting closer to Pennsylvania, Sarah began to have nightmares about her father. She would dream that she would find him on the battlefield seriously injured. She would call for help, but no one would answer or come to her aid. In her mind's eye, she would visualize him with some of the wounds that she had cared for during Chancellorsville.

She would wake up with the hollow feeling of not knowing where her father was or if he were still alive and unwounded. She couldn't imagine why she would have this same dream more than once. She was afraid that it meant that her father would be killed during the next battle.

She wanted to talk to Terrance about the dream but was afraid that he would not understand her fear. She had regular contact with him because when she had time, she helped with those who became sick on the march. She would often see him trying to talk some poor boy into going back to march with his company instead of riding along in the ambulance. She could almost hear the lecture he would be giving about being close to those who were seriously ill. "Now you know that you are well enough to march, and being around these sick men will make you feel more terrible and discouraged. Now be a good lad and go back to your company." Many times this would work, and the young man would become an effective soldier again.

Terrance was single-minded about keeping the sick from those who were wounded. He had seen so many times in the Crimea, and now in this war, the good effect of keeping the wounded clean and away from those carrying diseases. He was always encouraging Sarah with these words: "Stay clean, and be healthy."

Sarah didn't know if she agreed with everything he said, but it seemed that those wounded whom he cared for recovered faster and returned to their companies quicker.

Just as the army was entering Pennsylvania, Terrance came to her wagon, looking for a cup of hot coffee. As they spoke, Sarah brought up her dreams about her father. He thought for several minutes and then responded with a question. "Do you think of your father often during the days?"

"I worry about him because he seems so far away, and I haven't heard anything from him since before I left my Aunt Mary's home in February. That's months ago. I know that I can't expect to hear from him while I am with the Southern army, but that only adds to my worries."

"Most of the time when I have worried about someone far away, it turns out that I have worried over nothing. I think premonitions are bigger than reality, and sometimes far more devastating," he replied.

This was not what Sarah expected to hear, and it didn't give her any comfort. But it certainly did end the visit quickly. Terrance left with the excuse that he had to get back to the men he was taking care of.

One thing that Sarah realized was that she could not continue fretting about dreams. She determined to put that thinking out of her mind and concentrate on the day she was living. Remarkably, this didn't work. She still missed her father, and so she tried to picture him back on their farm with his mules and the work he loved.

She also missed her friends, especially Ralph and Minnie. She knew that Ralph had joined the Pittsburgh Iron Militia as soon as he turned eighteen. She also knew that he was anxious to fight and prove himself. He was like so many young men whom she had met— sure that death or injury would overlook them. She had also observed that no one knew for sure from one minute to the next in battle what could really happen. At the same time, Ralph was optimistic and full of young hope and courage. Sarah sometimes wondered if true courage was the ability to face overwhelming fear and continue to place one foot in front of the other. She had certainly seen that kind of courage plenty of times in the Southern army.

CHAPTER 23
1863, PENNSYLVANIA

Chauncey was assigned to be part of the scouting support for Early's Corps. He was constantly riding ahead of the main column, trying to determine what kind of reception the army would receive in the villages and hamlets along their line of march. To do all of this riding made him saddle sore and tired and wore down the horse he had bought from Abe Silver before Chancellorsville. He was always on the lookout for any sign that the huge Union army would be ahead of them, laying a trap for the men in gray to march into.

He had been one of the first of the gray army to cross into Pennsylvania. He quickly noticed the prosperous-looking farms and realized that the men would be happy at the prospect of eating well from the farmers of the North. He also realized that more and more, he longed for the old days when there was plenty in his father's house and on his father's table. He wondered how it would be after this campaign, when the war would end quickly after Lee broke the spirit of the North by marching across two Northern states and chasing Joe Hooker's army back to Washington, or beating them again in battle.

But for now, it would be grand to see all of the men well fed and ready for the hard fighting that Chauncey assumed would take place when they got close to the federal capital, which lay some miles to the east. That Lee had moved his army more than a hundred miles into Northern territory without any significant resistance amazed him and made him wonder if the North were capable of defending itself any longer. Naturally, Chauncey was untrained in military tactics, and he did not understand the danger in being overconfident while deep in the enemy's own territory. One day, he remarked to some of the men he rode with, "I believe we should be in Washington by the end of July."

Private Stoney, who had been in the war from the beginning and had survived a wound and the loss of an arm during the peninsular campaign, said to him, "Only if you're dressed in civilian clothes and working as a spy will you be in Washington by the end of July."

"What do you mean? We have passed through Maryland and are passing into Pennsylvania and have not seen any sign of gathering resistance. How can they stop us now?"

"You went to Aquia Creek and saw the massive buildup of supplies and munitions. You saw the boats coming in fully loaded with all manner of supplies. All of that was meant for an army that is likely twice the size of ours, with leaders who will one day know how to fight. How can you doubt that all of that will eventually roll right over the top of our Southern armies?"

Chauncey could not argue with what he had seen and reported. He could only think of the fighting spirit of the men he had been around for over two years, and he could only remember past victories. Stoney's words shocked him, especially coming from one who was brave enough to continue to fight, even though he had already given much to the Southern cause.

What Chauncey didn't realize was that the Northern army was moving north, shadowing Lee's army even as he entered Pennsylvania. The demoralized army that had been defeated at Chancellorsville was marching, ready to prove that they could recover and fight the Rebels on their own terms. In Washington, there was a command going out to change the leader of the Army of the Potomac, so Fighting Joe Hooker would be replaced.

The days on the march were becoming routine. Then, in late June, Chauncey showed up at Sarah's wagon and asked if she had any hot coffee and something to eat. By the looks of him and his horse, he had been traveling hard for some time. She had just started to cook some soup for a group of men that she had agreed to feed, and so she added some water to make enough for one more.

"You look like you haven't had any rest or a bath since we left Virginia."

"I haven't had a lot of time for that kind of relaxation. I have been scouting ahead with our small patrols, trying to figure out where the Yankees are," Chauncey answered.

"Where are they?" she asked.

"I haven't seen them, but I have seen dust over to the east that I think might be raised by a large army, and I have sensed that I'm being watched."

"Does that mean that you will be riding out again to make sure?"

"Maybe sometime tomorrow. Tonight I need to sleep."

Sarah determined that with that information she wanted to know more about what he was up to.

CHAPTER 24

1863, UNION MARCH TO PENNSYLVANIA

Sarah's father, Ted, had been with the Army of the Potomac since the beginning of the war and knew the hard, bitter lessons of retreat. The men in his company had been willing to fight, especially at Chancellorsville, but they were ordered to take up defensive positions before they had fired a shot. Then they were falling back, even though they had not yet seen any Confederate soldiers. The men knew that if the Southern army had been ordered to attack when the Union army was drawn up around the Rappahannock River, it would have been a horrible, bloody battle because they had the men and guns to beat the Rebels. But General Hooker ordered a retreat back to their original lines after some hard fighting that had involved not even half the army.

Now they were headed north across western Maryland, shadowing Lee's army from Northern Virginia. The men were tired of fighting hard and then retreating, and they wanted to show what they could do if given the chance. Some were aware that in the west, Grant had bottled up a large Confederate army at Vicksburg. If he could get them to surrender, then the Mississippi River would be controlled by the Union. That would mean that the Confederacy would not be able to reinforce or resupply west to east without taking a great risk.

Ted was tired of the war. He thought that it would be over in just a couple of years when the leaders in the South realized that they could not overpower the North. But he had underestimated the staying power of the Southern armies. He realized that it was largely a matter of leadership. Abraham Lincoln had changed commanding generals so often that some thought he was interfering too much in military affairs. Ted had to admit to himself at times that it seemed hopeless to try to bring an end to the war. However he had seen an increase in the size of the army, including the addition of former slaves and free Negroes. He had heard that when they were given a chance to fight, they gave a good account of themselves.

The night of June 28, as the army camped, the rumor spread that another general had been relieved. Ted now heard that "Fighting Joe Hooker" had been replaced by General Meade. So there it was again—another change at the top that the men would have to adjust to. Would this mean that they would now fall back on Washington, or would they continue to shadow the Confederate army and maybe try to bring on a battle where they chose, instead of where General Lee chose to fight? What would the orders be?

It only took two days for the new commander to be forced to move his troops very quickly toward the town of Gettysburg. He had planned on shadowing Lee's army until he made a decisive move, but General Buford had engaged the leading portion of one of the three columns of the Confederate army northwest of Gettysburg, and a battle was starting that neither General Lee nor General Meade wanted at that point. For the North, it seemed an appropriate time for the men to prove that they could win a battle in spite of what their commanding general had in mind.

From the beginning of the fighting, the Union army had been slowly forced back through Gettysburg past Seminary Ridge and finally to a good defensive position along Cemetery Hill and Culp's Hill. In this position, the Rebels would need to attack across mostly open ground, where the Union artillery would have open ranges of fire, and the men would have better cover than they had ever enjoyed before.

CHAPTER 25

THE NIGHT BEFORE GETTYSBURG

Sarah was more than curious about what Chauncey now did. He had lost command of the company of soldiers he had recruited because most of them would not follow him. He said it was because he was not from the South, but Sarah finally realized that there might have been other reasons. She decided to try to find out more about his activities while he was out of camp. She thought that he might be a traitor who could not be trusted. Since living in the North, she had become more ambivalent about the Southern cause, but she was convinced that if a person served in the army that he should be loyal to that service. As she became closer to the men and boys in the Southern army, she gained a strong affinity and affection for them as individuals and wanted to do anything to help them survive.

She decided she would follow Chauncey the next day when he rode out to scout, to see if he met with anyone suspicious or showed any signs of disloyalty.

The three corps of Lee's army were ordered to converge on the small town of Gettysburg. Union cavalry had been active in the area, and Lee wanted all of his army together just in case he was attacked by Meade's much larger force.

The next day, Chauncey was ordered to leave in the evening to try to see where the Union army was camping. General Early thought that he might be able to see from a distance many campfires that would be a sign of enemy activity.

Sarah was just finishing her nightly chores when she saw him getting ready to leave. On a strong impulse, she decided to follow him as far as she could. He was on horseback, so she didn't think she would be able to keep up very long. To her surprise, he was not moving fast because he was working his way through the Southern guards and pickets, not wanting to be observed. Sarah was able to follow him closely without his noticing her. She could tell he was riding southwest but did not know enough about the country to determine where she was. It was getting late, and the only real light came from the moon, which lit the trail they were traveling along but also created strange shadows in the trees and underbrush that thickly lined the road.

Then Chauncey stopped, as if listening to something. Because of the moonlight, Sarah could see well enough to note that he had taken off his hat and was turning his head side to side as if listening carefully or trying to see in the darkness. He then moved his horse back into the shadows, and she could no longer see him or the horse. As it grew later, she began to peer at his hiding place with more intensity. It almost looked like there was movement, but she could not make out if Chauncey was still where she had last seen him. Then she remembered the technique her father taught her when hunting—when it was too dark to see, she should use her ears and listen more intently. She slowed her breathing and concentrated on the night noises.

All Sarah could hear was a distant noise that sounded a little like small-arms fire. Could it be that the North and South had come together and started to skirmish? She did not know that Union and Confederate patrols had small firefights as they sporadically ran into each other. Both commanders were anxious to find out exactly where the main forces were located. She finally heard Chauncey's horse stomp and snort nervously, and then she heard the trotting of a horse coming from the southwest, along the trail Chauncey had been following. Then she heard Chauncey back his horse farther under a large tree.

As the rider approached, Chauncey called out for him to stop, telling the rider that he was surrounded. All Sarah could then hear was her own breathing and the stomping of the horse's hooves being kept under rein.

The rider replied, "If I am surrounded, show yourselves."

Chauncey seemed to hesitate for a moment, and then he said, "Martin, is that you?"

The other rider paused. "My name is Martin, and you sound like you grew up in Boston."

"Marty, it's Chauncey. I am trying to locate my company," Chauncey lied.

The two young men then walked their horses closer until they could see each other dimly in the dark. Chauncey had already dismounted, and then Marty, after getting a little closer, climbed down off his horse.

Marty said, "I know where I'm headed, but you look completely lost. In fact, I had heard that you were with the Rebels down in Virginia."

By this time, Chauncey had pulled out his revolver and taken careful aim at Marty. There was the distinct sound of the gun being cocked, and then Chauncey said, "I want you to put both hands on your horse's saddle. I am taking you prisoner."

Marty did as he was told, and Chauncey carefully got up behind him and pulled Marty's pistol from its holster.

Sarah could not believe that the two young men could meet by chance away from either army. She was moving closer, hoping to hear a little better what was being said, when she saw Marty slump to the ground. Then she saw Chauncey pick up a heavy rock from the ground and hit Marty's head as hard as he could. He then drew his sword and slashed at something before pulling a courier pack from Marty's body. At that point, Sarah realized that she was making noise coming through the trees and stopped suddenly. She saw Chauncey look toward where she was crouching by a large tree. He quickly mounted his horse and started toward her with his sword in hand, certain that she was a Yankee soldier. As he got close to her, he raised his sword, ready to strike. Sarah grabbed a low-hanging limb for support, swung her feet up, and kicked Chauncey's horse in the flank as hard as she could. The horse bolted just as he was swinging his sword, so instead of hitting her on the head or upper body, he hit her left hand, which was grasping the limb. The stroke severed the upper parts of her little finger and ring finger. Sarah felt an electrifying pain shoot up her arm, and she fell heavily to the ground.

Chauncey lost control of his horse when it bolted, and Sarah heard it running back along the lane toward where they had come from.

In spite of the pain in her hand, Sarah got up and went toward where Marty lay face down on the ground. She rolled him over and saw that he was not dead but certainly badly injured. She cradled his face close to hers, and she could tell that he was trying to say something. She said, "Marty, it's Sarah Clarke. I saw what Chauncey did to you."

Marty focused for a moment. "He's murdered me. Why?" With that, the light went out of his eyes, and he stared into the nothingness of death.

Sarah held him close and quietly started to weep. The pent-up tears came in a gush, and she sat with him for what seemed like an eternity. With a start, she recognized the clip-clop sound of another trotting horse and thought that Chauncey was returning to make sure he had finished her and Marty off.

She did not realize she was making any sound crying until she heard a Yankee voice quietly say, "What's happened here?"

She could only hold up her injured hand for protection. "He's been murdered."

Sam looked closely at the young woman and the dead trooper. He was sickened and shocked to recognize Marty. He leaned down close to Sarah and gently moved her arm back down as he looked closely at her. "Aren't you Sarah Clarke? What are you doing here?"

Sarah looked at him as carefully as she could and said, "Yes. Are you Marty's brother, Samuel?"

He managed to say yes, but that was all. He was now kneeling close to the two of them, and when he was finally able to speak, he said, "I would like to get him back to the main army so that he can be properly buried. Would you help me with him?"

His question seemed to jar Sarah back into the present and made her think about what she was doing. "I want to help, but my wagon and mules are back with Lee's army. I really should go back to take care of them."

Sam thought for a moment. "I don't want you to take the risk of being shot by an overexcited picket from either army. Please come with me so that I can make sure you are safe. There is going to be a battle close by here tomorrow. There have been sightings today of Confederate units, and General Reynolds has sent several couriers to General Meade requesting that he move his army forward with all speed. We hope that the rest of the Union army will move this way as fast as they can, and I am sure that there will be a big battle when the two armies meet. It is more important to move you to safety than to worry about your mules and wagon."

By this time, Sarah was trying to gently move Marty's body from her lap so that she could get up. When she did, her fingers started to throb so painfully that she thought she would pass out. "Please help me, Sam" was all she could say. Then she sat back down on the ground and started to weep again.

Sam knelt beside her and asked what was wrong. It was as much as she could manage, to raise her left hand. He very quickly examined the injured hand. He noticed that it was still bleeding and realized that she might possibly faint from shock and loss of blood.

"The first thing we need to do is stop the bleeding from your fingers. I have some bandages in my saddle kit."

Sarah was aware enough to remember that Terrance would certainly tell her to clean the wound first. She asked Sam if he had any whiskey or bourbon.

"I didn't think that you were a drinker, and I don't want to be the one to help you if you are."

"It's to clean my fingers, not to drink," she said.

As fast as he could, he retrieved his saddle kit. He pulled out the small flask of whiskey that he carried and a rolled-up piece of cloth he could use to bandage her wound. Then, as carefully as he could, he tied Marty's body over his own horse. He put Sarah in the saddle, and he climbed up behind her.

It took only a short time to discover the leading elements of the men rushing to Gettysburg. Sarah and Sam were sent to the back of the column where the medical people were bringing up the rear. Sam left Sarah and Marty's body with them and went back to the front.

CHAPTER 26
1863, GETTYSBURG

Sarah's father, Ted, and his company were dug in on the north side of Cemetery Hill. By noon of the second day's fighting at Gettysburg, they had already suffered heavy casualties. His good friend Ralph had been wounded just as the fighting started and had been evacuated to the rear where there was a farm with a large house and barn. The house was being used to treat the men as they came from the front, and the barn was filled with those who were waiting to have their wounds treated and those who would either recover from or die of their wounds.

The unconscious Ralph was placed on the dirty floor of the barn, not far from where Sarah was now sleeping.

The coincidences were almost too many for Sarah to comprehend. She regained consciousness some time after Ralph, who was dying, was placed near her. If she had seen him, she would have known that her father was nearby, but instead, she wandered toward the rear entrance to the barn and started looking for anyone who would help her know why she was at a farm and hearing the sounds of battle again. This battle was fiercer than anything she could have imagined. The two largest armies were engaged in a struggle that was producing casualties at a rate the doctors could not keep pace with. There was no time for anyone to help a lone, disoriented girl from the South.

Sarah looked around and then collapsed under a large oak tree next to some men whose wounds were not critical. They were resting, waiting for someone to care for them. She fell asleep again and slept until early evening, when the battle was all but over for the day. When she awoke, she was aware of the pain in her hand. She took off the bandage to see that it had stopped bleeding but was black from the bruising that Chauncey's sword had caused when he struck the blow.

As she looked at the fingers, she finally started to remember witnessing the murder of her young friend, and she started to weep again, thinking of his dying question. She only had hazy memories of the ride with Sam and the days since.

She realized that she needed to rewrap the wound to protect it, and she tried to use the part of the bandage that was least covered with her blood. When she had done the best she could, she started to look around to see if there was anyone she could help. She instinctively knew that if she worked, it would help her deal with her pain and Marty's death.

Meanwhile, Ted's position at Cemetery Ridge had almost been overrun in the late afternoon. Only by the fiercest fighting was the Rebel attack thrown back. Ted had sustained a wound to his left shoulder. Near the end of that day, his wound was aggravated when the wall he was behind was hit by an exploding shell, sending a stone crashing into his weakened left arm. He passed out from the pain and woke during the night, feeling agony that would not let him move his arm. He had seen so many men lose their arms and legs in the two years that he had been with the army, and now he was afraid that he would lose his arm.

As he started to move about, he quickly noticed that he was quite alone. He did not know where he was and could not figure out which way to go. He lay still, listening for any sound that might indicate where he was or where he might find help. He looked around and noticed in the distance a flickering light that might be a campfire so he started to crawl toward it. He had not gone very far when the pain in his shoulder made him pass out again.

He awoke with a start, hearing a noise like someone was talking quite loudly, but through a pipe and at a great distance. As he became more focused, he looked around and saw the gray-clad troopers not more than thirty feet from where he lay. He realized that they were moving up a small hill, coming under small-arms fire. He did not want to wait around and find out if a cannonade were going to start up to stop them from going any farther. He started to crawl as fast as he could away from the direction he thought they had come.

That was a mistake because he crawled right into the line of another enemy column that was moving up the hill, and they took him prisoner immediately. He soon found out that they were part of a detachment that was on the flank of the main column that was making the attack. They were watching to make sure that the Yankees would not outflank their column in the middle of the attack. For this reason, they did not take him to the rear immediately but posted a very young man to watch him to make sure he did not get away.

As the battle progressed, it looked like the Rebel column would overrun the Yankee position on the east side of Cemetery Hill. If they were able to do that, then the Yankee line could be turned, and another defeat similar to Chancellorsville could take place. Ted had heard about that attack. Stonewall Jackson's men had attacked O. O. Howard's line on an unprotected flank and routed the whole right side of the Union line. He knew that the Union had a better overall leader now, and that would mean that the gray line would very soon come under heavy artillery fire, and reinforcements would be rushed up to help stop the enemy surge.

It only took about an hour to see the beginning of the retreat, and Ted knew that he had to take his chance for escape as the retreat gained momentum. He watched for the young soldier to become distracted enough and then slipped to a shallow ditch that led uphill toward the right flank of the Union line. He started to crawl, but the movement caused him so much pain that the going was slow. He feared that the retreating men would stumble across him and either retake him or just kill him on the spot. But as the rush backward continued to gain momentum, he realized that it was going so fast that no one was worried about anything except surviving, so he lay very still for what seemed like hours, waiting for the battle to end for the day.

It only remained to be seen if the Union forces would push back now that they had the apparent advantage of men and guns. If they did, they could force Lee to retreat to a defensive position or possibly even force him to surrender.

Now Ted hoped he would be found by his own men, who would certainly be looking for dead and wounded. He knew his chances would be better if he could get out of the ditch and to a position where he could stand or sit upright. It wasn't long before he passed out again.

CHAPTER 27

1863, GETTYSBURG

Sarah awoke on the third day of the battle and felt somewhat stronger, even though the pain in her fingers was still severe. She couldn't remember that it had been looked at by a young surgeon and carefully stitched. He told her at the time to watch it closely for signs of infection and gangrene. The only way she could get a little relief from the pain was to keep her hand elevated to the height of her shoulder, so she fashioned a sling that pulled the hand across her chest to the right side and raised it at the same time. This was tiring to wear but made the pain more tolerable. Then she set about doing what she could for the more seriously wounded men near her. She could manage to carry water and dip a cup, which helped to bring simple relief to some of the men. Others she saw made her cry, remembering that there was nothing she had been able to do for Marty. From a distance, she heard the sound of a mighty battle. She wondered if her Southern friends had broken the Yankee line yet, and if she would be able to return and find her wagon and mules. She also worried about her friends from Tennessee and

Pittsburgh and prayed that they all would come through the battle without serious injuries.

As she worked later into the afternoon, she realized that the sound from behind the hill had diminished to a few scattered shots, and with that, she also knew that the Southern army had not broken through anywhere near her.

Sam walked up behind her and said, "I think it's over for today."

Sarah jumped because he had been so quiet in his approach, and she was concentrating on trying to hear the sounds of battle.

"I didn't mean to startle you, but I have been looking for you for some time. I wanted to let you know that I found a good place to bury Marty. I thought you would want to see his grave."

Sarah saw the pain in his eyes and realized how Marty's death was touching him. There would be many families grieving, hearts broken, after the work of destruction was finished here in this three-day battle.

"I would like to come with you, Sam, Does that mean he is already buried?"

"Yes, I did it last night after the fighting had ended for the day. I don't know what tomorrow will bring, but both armies are in pretty bad shape. I don't know if there will be more fighting tomorrow. We may have a truce to gather the dead and wounded."

There was silence between them as they made their way north along a road that led to the east side of Cemetery Hill. As they climbed higher, the battlefield came into view, and in the distance, Sarah could see the gathering clouds of a storm. She could not see all of the Southern boys lying in the fields beyond the hill they were on, but she could see smoke from the campfires further in the distance. It almost blended in with the gathering clouds.

At the southwest corner of the cemetery that gave the hill its name, they came to a fresh grave with a simple cross. Sarah couldn't help but remember the night when she saw Chauncey kill Marty. She wept quietly for the sudden loss of a boy she had only known briefly during a hunt in the mountains. It seemed so long ago.

Sam noticed her weeping but did not know what to do except put his arm out to her. He was surprised when she responded by moving toward him and laying her head on his chest. He brought his arm over her shoulders in a comforting hug. He had never comforted a grieving woman like this, and all he could do was stand still while she took comfort from his presence and then composed herself.

Sam finally said to her, "Let's walk down to that camp at the bottom of the hill. I think there might be some men who could use our help."

She followed him as he made his way toward a barn that was being used by the medical corps as a hospital. When they got there, they were surprised at how closely packed the men were. There was hardly room to move between the rows of injured and dying men.

"Is there any way that we can help them?" Sarah asked Sam. There seemed to be no organization, just men crowded together with no regard to keeping the sick or dying separate from those who had sustained lesser injuries.

As they were talking about the conditions and what would be a logical solution, Sarah heard what sounded like her name being spoken nearby. She turned to look in the direction the voice was coming from, but she did not see anyone who would have called to her.

A few seconds went by, and she heard the call again, except this time, she could better see where the voice was coming from, and she recognized who it was. As she made her way toward the man, she saw the familiar look in his eyes, even though the face had changed with a beard and the effects of pain. It was her father, Ted, who had called out. She was almost overcome by the shock not only of seeing him but seeing him in these circumstances. She had hoped that he would escape injury, but as she neared him, she became very aware that his injuries were serious.

As surprised she was to see Ted, his amazement at seeing her in the barn was even greater, almost like seeing a ghost from the past. "You look so very much like your dear mother" were his first words. "God bless you. What are you doing here?" he asked.

She wanted to tell him the whole adventure but not with so many injured men so close by. Besides, the only thing she could think about was getting him out of the hospital. "I need to get you away from here," she said. "You need to be in a place where you can get better care."

Even though her father was against leaving those he had fought beside for the past two years, Sarah was finally able to convince him to let her take him away.

Sam quietly watched the reunion between them and then said to Sarah, "How do you propose to transport your father anywhere? There are no extra wagons or ambulances right now that can be spared for one man."

"If I can find my wagon and mules, will the army let me take him away?" she asked.

"I will ask for a furlough for him. I am sure that, in his condition, if there is a reasonable offer to take him, they will let him go. Do you know where to start looking for your wagon and mules?"

"After we passed through Gettysburg, we were on the pike to Harrisburg when the column was ordered to turn back and join the main army. I think if I start up that same road, I will find them—unless they were taken along with the army," she said.

"Chances are they are gone, but I can take the rest of today and tonight to help you look. After that, there are duties I need to take care of."

Sam went back to his campsite to get his horse and then picked Sarah up. The two of them tried to backtrack to where she thought Early and his men had come from. It took them the rest of the day to find her wagon, which was just where she had left it, but there was no sign of the mules. Mattie was standing just a short way from the wagon.

"I thought it was best to let them wander," Mattie said without being asked. "When the men came by in the morning before the battle looking for you, I told them that you were out looking for the mules, and we would catch up."

Sam was taken aback that this young Negro woman would speak so boldly to them, and then Sarah said, "Sam, I want you to say hello to my friend, Mattie. She has been with me almost since I left Cleveland, and she, like me, was traveling to the army around Fredericksburg. She saved me and has become a wonderful friend."

Sam still looked incredulous but managed to stutter a brief hello. Then he looked questioningly at Sarah.

Sarah looked in the box of her wagon where she kept a special whistle that she used to call the mules when she couldn't find them. Usually, the most effective way to locate the mules was to let them find her. She blew the whistle for about ten minutes trying to turn in all directions. Then the three of them sat down to rest and wait.

"If they are close enough to hear the whistle, then they should be here within an hour or two," Sarah said. "We might as well light a fire and cook some food and brew some coffee while we wait. I can cook beans with some salted pork that I have in the wagon. The army must have moved out awfully fast to have overlooked the food in my wagon."

"Sarah, we need to be able to get back by tomorrow morning for me to be able to report. I can't spend too much more time here, or my commander will think I have gone missing," Sam said.

"I just want to give the mules time to come back. If you need to leave, don't worry about us. We are fine on our own," she said, "but let's at least eat something first."

There was not much conversation as they waited for the fire to first heat up and then for the food to cook. Each was thinking about the remarkable coincidences of the past week that had brought them all together and reunited Sarah with her father.

Sam finally asked why Sarah had been out by herself the night she found Marty, and what had happened to her fingers. It was obvious that the circumstance was one she did not care to talk about, but he pressed her, feeling he had a right to know all she knew about his brother's death.

"Sarah, I think you need to tell me why you were near Gettysburg the night Marty was killed. Now that we have found your wagon, it is obvious that you had gone some distance without it, either on horseback or foot. Please tell me what you know about Marty's death."

Sarah thought for a few moments and decided to tell him everything except who killed Marty. She wanted to know if Chauncey was still alive before she reported his involvement. She was confused about why he would do what he did and about her own feelings for him. There were times during the last few months when she thought she knew and loved him, and other times when he seemed like a complete stranger and someone she did not want to know. She was conflicted because of her feelings for Marty and Chauncey.

"There was a man. I was following him to find out what he was doing. He was supposed to be a scout for our army, but I thought he might be a spy for the Yankees. He was so strange in his habits. I know I had no business following him, but I wanted to know if he was a hero or a villain. He was not traveling fast and would often dismount and walk his horse, probably to be able to see and hear better. After what seemed like two or three hours, he stopped and took his hat off. Then I was able to hear a single rider coming along the road. When the rider was close enough, he called out for him to stop, telling him that he was surrounded and was being taken captive.

"The man I was following told the rider that he was fairly captured, and he had him dismount. They were talking low for a few minutes, and I was able to move close enough to suspect that I had heard the voice of the rider before, but I wasn't sure. At that point, the man I was following told Marty that he could ride on. Marty turned to mount his horse, and it was then that the man I was following hit Marty from behind. It shocked me so much that I must have cried out. The man I was following quickly had his sword out. He cut off a pouch that Marty was carrying and then got on his horse and turned toward me. I was sure he was going to kill me and all I could think to do was to use the tree I was behind for protection. As he came at me, I moved around the tree, grabbed an overhead limb, and swung up and kicked his horse as hard as I could. He swung his sword just as the horse bolted and cut off the end of my fingers.

"I don't know how long it took me to get to Marty, but it seemed like a long time. When I got to him, I recognized him and knew that he was badly injured. I wanted to give him water or do something, but all he could do was ask why the man had murdered him. Then he died. I don't know how long afterward you came, but I thought it was the man coming back to kill me.

"I couldn't believe what I had seen, and I couldn't believe it was you who came along. What were you doing out on your own that night?" she asked Sam.

"Marty and I had planned to ride back to Meade's headquarters together. It was his first time riding as a courier, and I was going to make sure he was OK. He left sooner than we had planned, and I tried to catch up to him but was too late."

As they were talking about the events of that night, they heard the nearby braying of one of the mules. A moment later, they heard the second mule answering from a little farther away. Then Sarah whistled again, and both mules trotted into their camp.

"It amazes me that you have that much control over your mules," Sam said.

"They are so smart that you have to gain their trust before you can train them. Even then, they are as stubborn as any human and need to know who is boss before they will be obedient," she answered.

"When we were on the hunting trip with you, your father he told me that you could do a lot more with your mules than he could. He said you had a gift."

"It's funny with them," she answered. "You never know when they will finally learn something that you are trying to teach them. My father said that I had a gift with them, but I think it's that they know I love them and would never deliberately hurt them."

"Do you feel strong enough to return to Gettysburg with me now?" Sam asked.

"I think I can make it. Will you help Mattie hitch the mules to the wagon?" she asked.

As they traveled back toward the camp where she had left her father, Sarah began to plan how best to take care of him. She thought about taking Mattie with her, and then she decided to leave it up to her whether or not to go along. It was clear to her that a trip to their home in Cleveland would be dangerous and would take them through Confederate territory. She decided to try to return with Ted to Pittsburgh. She thought that Mrs. Baxter would be able to help—and would probably want to help.

CHAPTER 28

1863, PITTSBURGH, PENNSYLVANIA

As Sarah pulled the wagon up in front of the Baxter home, she saw Mrs. Baxter on the front porch, rocking slowly in her chair. She looked so melancholy that Sarah hesitated to call to her. Before she could, Mrs. Baxter looked up and recognized Sarah immediately. She called out, "Oh, Sarah, is that really you?"

"Yes, it is, and I have Father in the wagon. He was hurt in the battle at Gettysburg. He told me what happened to Ralph. I am so sorry."

"I just received word yesterday. I have not known what to do. It must have been a horrible battle, but what are you doing with your father? And it looks like you have picked up a friend on the way."

Sarah got down from the wagon and went up onto the porch with Mrs. Baxter before she started to talk. "Mattie, this is Mrs. Baxter, a very good friend. Mrs. Baxter, this is Mattie." Turning to Mattie, Sarah said, "What is your surname, Mattie? You have never said."

"When Mr. McFarland filled out the paper acknowledging my freedom, he wrote 'Matilda McFarland' for my name. No one has ever used it. People always just called me Mattie."

Then Sarah, without explaining about how she came to be at Gettysburg, said, "The army let me take Father because there were so many wounded. I think having one man less in the hospitals was a tiny relief to them. It's taken us five days to get here because I wanted to go slow so that Father's wounds would not start to bleed again. I was hoping that you might tell me where I can take him so that I can be with him while he recovers."

"Yes, I can, child, You can bring him through that front door and put him in Ralph Junior's room. I won't hear of you staying anywhere else."

"But I don't want to burden you right now any more than you are, and I know that Father would feel awkward about staying without Ralph being here."

Sarah did not hear her father approach, but he had managed to get out of the wagon while she was talking to Mrs. Baxter and to walk unsteadily up the path to the porch. "Mrs. Baxter, I have a letter for you from Ralph that he wrote before the second day of the battle when he was killed. He asked me to get it to you. We often exchanged letters before going into battle, for each other's loved ones, just in case one survived without the other."

He handed the bloodstained envelope to Mrs. Baxter and then leaned heavily against the porch pillar.

"Please come inside and let me have a few minutes alone while I read this," she said.

Mrs. Baxter left the three of them in Ralph's room while she went to the kitchen to read the letter. It was a letter mainly filled with practical instructions about their savings and other matters she would need to know about the house and farm. It ended with two paragraphs that were far more personal and sacred to her than she would ever want to share with anyone.

By the time she returned to Sarah, Mattie, and Ted, she was composed and very determined to see them comfortably situated in her home. "Sarah, you can share the bed with Minnie for now. I know she will be thrilled to see you and find out what you have been doing since you left us last fall. Mattie, I would like you to share my room if you would, especially if you will tell me how you have come to be with Sarah. Ted, you can stay here as long as you need or want to. With your injuries, will you need to return to the army?"

At that point, Ted was so exhausted that he was unable to respond with anything in a coherent way, so the three women made him comfortable in the bed and went out to see to the mules and wagon. Sarah drove the wagon behind the house, where there was a comfortable barn with a stable and a place to leave the wagon.

As they finished, Mrs. Baxter said to Sarah, "I need some help now. Are you any good with a hammer and crowbar?"

"I've been around our barn at home all my life and have always loved using all the different tools to help with my father's work."

"Good, because in Ralph's letter he suggested some things that I could do with the money we had been saving over the years. We kept it in a steel box in the barn where we thought it would be safer than in a bank. He never really trusted banks, and we have never been sorry for always having control of our own money."

Sarah laughed at that. "I can see why he and my father were such good friends, because if you were in Tennessee now, and our positions were reversed, I would be saying the same thing to you. Even though my uncle owns a bank in Knoxville, my father would not trust him with very much of our money and certainly not any of the gold coins he saved."

Mrs. Baxter gave Sarah a knowing look and motioned for her to follow. Together, they swept away the dust and dirt that had accumulated in the middle of the barn floor, and underneath the dirt, they found a yellow-painted board. "Is it under that board?" Sarah asked.

"No, that is just the starting point for the directions to the hole where the box is kept." From that board, Mrs. Baxter counted north five boards and then placed the pitchfork pointing east down on the fifth board. At the tip of the pitchfork, there was another plank that, when pried up, revealed a heavy steel box with a lock in the lid. When Mrs. Baxter removed the lock, they had to place an iron bar through a loop in the lid, and this allowed the two of them to force the lid from the box. The box held more than just gold coins. It also contained the deeds to other properties that the couple owned in Pittsburgh.

Mrs. Baxter was somewhat chagrined when she looked at the deeds and remembered that she should have been collecting rent payments from the businessmen who were leasing property from her and Ralph. Ralph had normally collected the rents just after the first of each year, but this had not been done since he had left for his service in the war, so two years of rent were now owing.

She removed a few coins from the box. Then the two women replaced the lid, and the steel box was locked and hidden again under the plank in the barn.

Mrs. Baxter told Sarah that she and her husband had agreed years before that the banks might be good places to hold certain funds, but they should always have a supply of hard money hidden away that they could use when they needed. She was somewhat worried that the people who were renting their stable and barn had either forgotten that they owed for the time they used the property, or they were unable to pay, or worst of all, they were going to try not to pay now that Ralph was gone. She would go the next day, see what the situation was, and try to collect at least some of the amount owing.

Sarah was more concerned about the rooms she and her father were using and the food that they would be consuming. "Mrs. Baxter, I know that my father would want me to pay you for the food and housing costs. He would feel much easier in his mind, and it would help him recover sooner if he knows that I have taken care of that expense."

"Sarah, you know that you are welcome here and that I love you like my own child. Taking care of your father gives me a connection to my poor, dead husband, and I know that his ghost would come back and haunt me if I took money from his friend. Part of the letter he sent me via your father told of his love for him. They were closer than if they had been brothers. If you will be a true friend to both of my children, it will do more than any amount of money you would pay."

"You know I already love Minnie and Ralph. They are the brother and sister that I never had before. But I believe Father will still feel very awkward about staying without helping with the expenses."

At this point, Mrs. Baxter realized that Sarah wanted to feel some measure of control and responsibility for the care of her father. She was wise enough to put off the decision about money until both of them had time to move past the emotions that had come to the surface and had already caused both women to shed more tears in the past few days than ever before in their lives.

CHAPTER 29
1863, A NEW WAR

Sarah, Mattie, and Ted stayed at the Baxters' house for several weeks before he was able to move around enough to start to regain his strength. He had lost his left arm almost up to the elbow and was impatient to learn to live without it. It was not the best time for Sam to show up with a proposal for Sarah, but that's just what happened.

Sarah had been away shopping with Mrs. Baxter and didn't know that Sam was there, having a discussion with Ted about her immediate future.

Sam had explained to Ted more about how he had found Sarah kneeling over the body of his youngest brother. He remembered that she had said she wished that she could be of some use in shortening the war so that more men and boys would not die.

"Ted, did she ever tell you how she came to be with Lee's army at Gettysburg?" Sam asked.

"She would only say that Chauncey showed up at my sister's in Knoxville and overwhelmed Herbert, Mary, and her with his charm. He was so convincing that the South was on the verge of great victories and that Sarah would have an opportunity to be part of that. He told them that he would make sure that Sarah would always be in a safe place, away from the fighting. I also believe that Herbert would have tried to persuade her to go with Chauncey because if I die and something happens to Sarah, then Mary will inherit our farm and anything else I own."

"So much for his promises," Sam replied. "She would not tell me anything about the person she was following, and yet she had pursued him so far from her wagon and mules, that after the battle was over, it took us hours to find them again."

Ted looked thoughtful for a moment. "She would only tell me that she was following a man that she thought might be a traitor and that she would let Chauncey know about it. I am certain that neither of us have the complete story yet."

Both men sat together, quietly thinking about the events of the past few weeks and trying to make the most of the information they had.

Finally, Sam broached the subject that had brought him all the way to Pittsburgh. "After seeing how far she followed the person who injured her, and what kind of country she was in, I would like to approach her about helping me with my work with the army. I have been assigned to be the chief of civilian scouts for Rosecrans's army in Tennessee. We have some people who gather any information that would be useful for our planning. Sarah told me that she had been cooking for a group of men from Tennessee and also that she had been helping with the wounded during and after the battle at Chancellorsville. I would like to get your permission before I talk to her. I assure you that I will not mention the subject unless I have your approval. I am being transferred to work with Rosecrans's army, so she would be back in Tennessee."

Ted was amazed that Sam would think of Sarah for such a position until Sam explained that she was more familiar with the area around Chattanooga than anyone else he knew and could trust. She would not give the information directly to anyone that might be working for the Union. There was a blacksmith in Cleveland, Tennessee, who had been wounded while fighting for the South, but he had changed his sympathies while in a Union hospital. He now gave as much information to the North as he could find.

"Sam, I didn't know anything about her leaving Knoxville. I missed her letters when she left here, and she admitted that she had not bothered to write to tell me about going with Chauncey. If she had asked me, I would have said no."

He was now heartsick at the thought that Sam wanted to use her as a spy. "Let us talk to her together to see how she would feel about going back home. I will discourage her as much as possible as I am sure you will try to talk her into the scheme," Ted said.

As Sarah entered the room, she could feel the tension between the two men and wondered what could have possibly caused it. Then, she heard Sam's offer to go to Chattanooga and to do there basically what she had been doing with Lee's army in Virginia: that is, work with Bragg's confederate army to help with cooking, supplies, and nursing the wounded. As she would be working with the wounded, she could gather information from them about what corps they were with and where they thought they would be going. Whenever she had information she needed to pass along, she could go to Cleveland where there was a man who had a stable, and she could give the information to him. Sam then told her he was convinced the war would be over as soon as the Southern leaders realized that all they were doing was prolonging the inevitable by continuing to resist the power of the North.

Sarah was stunned that Sam would consider her for such a role. She couldn't imagine what made him think that she would be part of any scheme to help the North. She had already seen quite a bit more danger than she anticipated when Chauncey talked her into going with his group. Even though she had not explained to anyone whom she had been following that night just outside Gettysburg, she knew how quickly a person you trusted could turn and try to kill you.

"Father, are you in favor of this plan for me just because it would help the Union?" she asked.

Ted was taken aback by the question. "I am letting Sam make the proposal because he is so earnest about it. I myself would rather that you remain here with me until I am well enough to go back into the army, and then I'd like you to return to Knoxville to live with Mary."

"I didn't know you were even thinking about getting well enough to go back," she said. "What makes you think that they would want a one-armed man back in the ranks?"

"You forget that I was promoted to the rank of colonel. I would not be carrying a musket or rifle but would be using a sword and revolver. I believe that I can still help, maybe in ways that I would not have been able to before I was wounded. There are plenty of men and officers who have been seriously wounded but come back and make a good contribution to our effort because they are not only experienced but more dedicated. The reason I am not in favor of you going to work for Sam and his spies is that I cannot stand the thought of you going into danger again."

Sarah thought about this for some time. Then Sam broke the silence with a comment that made Sarah think that he was finally thinking more of her welfare than his duty.

"I can appreciate your father's concerns, Sarah, and I cannot promise that you would not be hurt or killed. This war has taken so many lives suddenly without reason. There have been so many civilians killed unexpectedly that no one, soldier or civilian, can know if he will survive. Both armies know that there are spies but have been mostly tolerant toward them. However, when some civilians find there are spies in their midst, there have been lynchings and other atrocities committed against those they suspect."

"Sam, how soon do you need an answer? Do I have any time to think about this and talk more with my father? Will you give me a day or two, please?"

Sam thought that was only right and said he would return either the next day or the day after so that they could have a complete discussion of the issues. "But if that is not enough time, I can be reached through the war department. General Halleck has a special clerk assigned to the civilian scouts. So really, you have enough time to see that your father is well and decide if this is something you really want to do."

As he was leaving, Mrs. Baxter stopped him on the front porch and asked how long it had been since he had eaten a good, home-cooked meal, and she insisted that he return the following evening for supper. He was only too willing to accept the invitation. Army food was not only bad, but it could sometimes be unhealthy.

The next evening when Sam went to the Baxter home, he found another person there he did not expect. The son Ralph had come home on leave. He had been told about Sam's proposal and was completely against Sarah going along with it. After they had been introduced, he asked Sam to go outside with him for a few minutes so that he could try to talk him out of the idea.

"Sam, I can't believe that you would even think that she could feel safe enough to join in with this harebrained scheme. She has been up with her father most of the night discussing the idea and how she might help. Sarah said that she knew a woman who was in uniform with the Southern army and was brave enough to stand by her husband and fight at Fredericksburg. Even after her husband was killed, the woman fought at the battle at Chancellorsville, and that's while she was pregnant with his baby. So now Sarah thinks that she should do something just as reckless because her father has been wounded."

"Ralph, I was ready to give up on the idea when I left last night, and now I feel foolish for even approaching her father about it. I will do what I can to talk her out of it, short of withdrawing the offer. I don't know what emotions have been stirred up, but I need to tell you that I believe she has unique abilities that would not only make her valuable but would also keep her as safe as possible. I have tried to think of her father's perspective, and that is why I will give them all the time they need for her to decide. We could also use someone like you to come along and work as a courier. Then you could at least stay in touch with her, if she decides to do this."

That was the last thing that Ralph thought would come of this discussion. He thought that they might have settled their differences behind the barn if Sam did not listen to reason, but now he was overcome by this completely new twist. He certainly lost control of that situation faster than General Hooker at Chancellorsville.

"Let's go inside, Ralph. Your mother promised me a home-cooked meal, and to tell the truth, that is the only reason I am here this evening."

During dinner, Sam was able to observe firsthand a family that was as close as his own. He saw that even though they had suffered the great loss of Ralph Baxter, there was a strong bond among the family members and their friends, and that they all had hope in the future. His own conscience had been so torn because of the loss of Marty that he had been in a blue funk since the end of the battle at Gettysburg. He had been performing his duties from reaction more than planning. Being in this wonderful home helped him start to heal from his guilt and sorrow.

The talk around the table did not center on his plan for Sarah. Instead, they talked about mundane, everyday news and events in cities far away. Mostly they enjoyed the quiet of being in a safe place, and the war seemed, for that short time at least, to be very far away.

At the end of the evening, Ralph, Minnie, and Mrs. Baxter went into the parlor while Sarah and Ted said their good-byes to Sam.

"Sarah, I do not want to pressure you to make a decision. The way that most of the Union generals plan things, it may be that we will all be too old to help before they move," Sam said.

Ted laughed quietly as Sarah looked at Sam and said, "There was never any doubt that I would eventually accept the job. Once we started to talk last night, after you left, all I had to do was remind my father that I had already survived living in the same house with his brother-in-law, and he realized that I am far more capable of subtle deception than he was giving me credit for. Mostly, we talked about traveling arrangements to get me and my mules first to our farm in Cleveland and then to Bragg's army. I also wanted to make sure that Mattie knew she was welcome if she wanted to come along. She and Mrs. Baxter have already become so close. Mattie said that she had not felt this safe since she was with Mr. and Mrs. McFarland together in Bermuda, so I think she would like to stay here with her. But before I leave, I want to make myself as useful as possible to my father in his recovery and to the Baxters. How much time do I have before I am needed?"

"As President Lincoln says, most of the Union generals have the 'slows.' It takes them a long time to get organized and collect all of the equipment they need, and Rosecrans appears to be no different. Your father could be retired before Rosecrans leaves his comfortable lodgings to move toward Bragg's army in Chattanooga. When you are available to come, get word to me through General Halleck in Washington. We can make travel arrangements better when we know where the armies are located and can plan the route based on getting you safely there. I asked Ralph if he would like to transfer to our service and become a courier for us. I don't know what he will decide, but I am hoping he will join me when I leave. If not, I will give him the same information about contacting me through General Halleck."

As he gathered himself to leave, Sam reflected on the turn of events in this evening's conversations. When he first approached the house before dinner, he was determined that he would just enjoy the company and food and would not even bring up the idea of bringing Sarah onto the side of the North as a civilian scout. Now it looked like she would and even her friend Ralph would consider the transfer. He sincerely hoped he had not made a mistake in asking either of them and that they would not be placed in any more danger than they had been facing the past six months.

CHAPTER 30

1863, CHATTANOOGA, TENNESSEE

S arah arrived in Cleveland in October and stopped at the farm. She found that the house had not been lived in, even though Chauncey's father had leased the property. Most of the single farm workers had left either for the army or to find work. Harry and Smitty were both still away with the army, and their wives were still living in the cottages on the farm. Sarah was so happy to see them that she thought for a moment that she would not go on to meet Bragg's army but would spend the rest of the war in her own home and with these wonderful friends. She realized though that she had promised both her father and Sam that she would do what she could to gather information and pass it along, although she didn't know what she could possibly learn that would help.

By the time she arrived, Bragg's Southern army was in a commanding position around Chattanooga and had the Union army cooped up in the town, where they were on starvation rations. They had beaten Rosecrans's forces during the battle of Chickamauga and had forced them back to Chattanooga, where they were cruelly trapped and did not see a way to break the siege.

When Sarah finally came to Bragg's army, she found that even though they had the Union army trapped, they were themselves in dire circumstances. The food was inadequate, and the men were ill clothed and sleeping in tents that would not keep out the cold of the late fall nights. The generals of the several divisions were barely on speaking terms with their commander and had petitioned President Davis to remove Bragg from overall command of the army.

Even though Sarah found conditions so pitiful as to make a mother weep, the boys and men retained an outrageous sense of the ridiculous that often showed itself in odd ways. When she arrived one day with a wagonload of flour that she intended to share with some other cooks, one of the young soldiers said, "What's in the wagon, missy? Looks like a lot of white bags full of air!"

"Flour for baking," she responded.

"Is that flour fortified, so's we'll be stronger?"

"I am sure that it will help you fight better when the time comes."

"Then it must be fortified with gray weevils, cause them blue ones are downright weak."

She thought for a moment then said, "No, I think these are Bragg weevils so that they will make everyone mad enough to fight."

They shared a good laugh, and then he helped her take the flour to a dozen different cooks.

Sarah was cooking for a part of Longstreet's corps that had some Tennessee volunteers. She had settled in with them to help gather supplies and do whatever else she could that would make their lives more tolerable. This turned out to be a great benefit to the men because Sarah knew the surrounding country well, and with that knowledge, she could gather food and other supplies more efficiently than others who were assigned to the same task.

One day in early November, she heard that the plan was to send Longstreet's corps to Knoxville to try to take the town from Burnside, who had driven out the Confederates in the first part of September. The city was vital to the South because the railroad connection from Tennessee to Richmond carried a lot of the food supplied from the west, and that helped feed people in Richmond and the armies that were nearby.

She left for Cleveland as soon as she could to inform her contact of this planned movement of a corps from Bragg's besieging army. She didn't know it at the time, but this was likely the most important information that she would ever furnish to the new Union commander, General Ulysses Grant. She visited with the blacksmith, Elmer Pointer, while he was putting new shoes on her mules and gave him the information.

"I am sure that General Grant has already heard rumors of the planned move, but your information will confirm it and make it possible for him to use his men more effectively in breaking the siege," Elmer said. "I will pass it along to Ralph as soon as I can."

If Sarah had known that there was someone watching her closely, she would not have felt so comfortable about her planned return to the army that day. She had been in Cleveland overnight gathering supplies, and she intended to leave as soon as the work on the mules was finished. Across the lane in a stand of trees, there was a gray figure, hardly moving and watching her intently.

Sarah said her good-byes before noon and left for Chattanooga. The weather was cool and the air crisp with the smells of the earth going to sleep for the winter. It brought back memories of the hunt three years ago when she had such a grand time with Marty and his brothers—and Chauncey. The day turned suddenly gloomy when she recalled Marty's last words and realized she would never see him again. She seemed to get a clearer sense of what it meant to the families who had lost loved ones, the pure sadness of the loss of precious fathers, sons, and brothers. She wondered what would happen when the war was over, and the living remembered the dead and the unbelievable price that had been paid in the name of Union and freedom. Some would be freer than before, and others less so. She had a clear picture in her mind of the many dead and dying, and the maimed and crippled. So many young men would have a much harder time surviving because of the limitations caused by the loss of arms and legs. Then she thought of Marion and wondered where she was and what she was doing. By now, she must have had her baby, and hopefully she would be in either her family's home or Edmond's.

For a good portion of the trip back to camp, Sarah was preoccupied with these thoughts of the past and what it would mean to her future life. She was suddenly brought back to reality when she heard the clip-clop of a horse's hooves approaching from behind her. She turned around and saw the horse was still far enough behind that all she could make out was the gray color of the soldier's clothing. The horse was very much the color of the white horse Chauncey had been riding when they were traveling through the mountains in the late winter. When she saw the rider, she had a sudden urge to whip up her mules to speed, to race as fast as possible back to the camp. She realized that the mules pulling the wagon would be no match for a mounted rider determined to catch her. She made sure that she still had the cavalry pistol Ralph Baxter had given her just before she left Pittsburgh. He said that if she were intent on risking her life, she might as well have some protection against anyone trying to do her harm. She knew very well how to shoot a musket and rifle, but she was not sure she could hit anything with the pistol. She might need to rely on bluff more than skill in the event she pulled the big gun.

It took about ten minutes for the rider to get close enough to hail her, and so it seemed that he was not necessarily intent on doing her harm. She was more than surprised when he called, "Sarah Clarke, is that really you?"

She tugged on the reins and applied the wagon brake to bring it to a stop. The voice and tone were vaguely familiar, and she was curious about who was hailing her.

As she turned in her seat to get a better look, she realized that even a short time could make enough of a difference in someone's appearance that he became unrecognizable. She could not tell that this bearded young man had been with the group of recruits with whom she had first traveled to Virginia.

"I am sorry," she said. "Your voice is familiar, but I don't recognize you."

Her heart sank as she recognized the voice when he said, "You should remember your first tormentor, Clarence Taylor. I'm his brother, Amos. He will be more than happy that you have been found."

Sarah could hardly collect her thoughts and emotions as she began looking for a way to escape this unplanned meeting. She could only think to ask the most obvious question. "What are you doing here?"

Amos smiled. "When we had to suddenly leave that recruiting group, I was able to quickly convince Clarence that the worst thing we could do was run for home. So as soon as we could, we turned east, found our way to Richmond, and heard that Longstreet was collecting supplies somewhere around Suffolk. We headed that direction and joined up with him. We missed the fight at Chancellorsville but were in on Gettysburg and then Chickamauga. I know that you are probably wary of letting me travel along back with you, but I assure you that I am not anything like my brother, Clarence."

Under the circumstances, this last comment gave Sarah little comfort, but she did not really know how to respond. "Are you still with Longstreet's corps?"

"Yes, Clarence has been promoted to lieutenant and is one of the leaders of my company. This is the horse that he took the night we left in a hurry. He had to sell it to the colonel and at the same time promise to take care of it. Then he was suddenly given his promotion. Now I take care of the colonel's horse, and he lets me use it occasionally. The fighting has changed Clarence, and I am sure he would like a chance to apologize to you for what he did. We leave soon for the

North, and with the fighting being what it is, this could be his last chance to clear his conscience."

This didn't necessarily have the effect on Sarah that Amos might have intended. She really had put the past behind her and did not want to be reminded of the sordid incident. She had some satisfaction in knowing that Clarence had whooped with pain when Mattie hit him, and if he apologized, it might reduce that satisfaction somewhat. She did not necessarily feel that confident in Amos's protests that he was not like his brother. In her mind, he was contaminated by association. But there was not a clear reason that she felt she could give for refusing, so she started up again with him riding alongside.

When they were about a mile from the camp, Amos spurred his horse ahead, and she was relieved that she would enter the area alone. She was very surprised when she approached the first line of pickets and saw that there was a group of men waiting for her. She knew that the supplies she always brought back generated a lot of interest, but she had never had a welcoming committee. Then she recognized Clarence. He was beside Amos, astride the horse that he had taken from Chauncey. The only change she saw in him was the pronounced scar just above his nose in the middle of his forehead. Clarence smiled at her, pulled out his revolver, and told her to get down from the wagon. Then, addressing another officer who was next to him, he said, "I believe that this is the spy that Amos just told us about."

Sarah could not have been more taken aback if he had offered an apology for his behavior last spring. She did not know what to say because she had just that morning passed along to Elmer Pointer the information that confirmed Longstreet's orders to move out for Knoxville. She flushed so red and was so angry at being caught so easily that she barely comprehended what the officer said to the men.

"Put your pistol away, Lieutenant. We will not be hanging anyone today, especially not this young girl."

Sarah was almost equally angry at being called a young girl, but at the same time, she was relieved to hear the captain's tone. She recognized in it that same kind of chivalry the colonel had used with Lieutenant Stevens when he wanted to court-martial Marion after Chancellorsville.

"I doubt that she has given any information to the Federals that they haven't already heard from our own pickets when they were busy trading tobacco for coffee."

In this, the captain was mistaken, for she had informed Elmer of the transfer of Longstreet's corps almost as soon as the order was given. General Grant was delighted to hear the news but could do nothing with it until Sherman had his men in place to attack Bragg's northern flank.

"But does that mean that we should not make an example of her so that our men will stop their fraternizing?" Clarence asked. "I am sure she has been spying for the North almost from the first day she was invited to travel with us recruits."

This was a shock to Sarah, and then she wondered why Clarence had come to the conclusion that she was now a spy. This was all happening so fast that she could not even begin to think what she would offer as a response if she were asked about the facts.

The captain, on the other hand, thought that Clarence's accusations were a complete fantasy brought on by his weak imagination. Still, he was ready to make a token example of Sarah by exiling her from the Southern front.

"We will send her away so that she won't do any more damage, but I don't see the point in wasting our time trying to make an example that will be forgotten the first time our men are tempted to trade secrets for something they want. Besides, I don't think it will help us win a battle or a war if we start hanging young women. I personally know of a spy in Richmond who runs a very successful spy ring and is well known for doing so. Nevertheless, she still roams the streets freely, supposing that everyone thinks she is a little crazy. There is no talk of hanging her."

The captain turned to Sarah. "Young woman, you are now forbidden from entering our lines while we are here or anywhere else. You may think that you have helped the Union army, but if you look closely at the positions here on Missionary Ridge and Lookout Mountain, you will understand why General Bragg said he could hold this ground with half the number of men that he has under his command. He also believes that he can reestablish the stranglehold on the Federal supply line into Chattanooga."

Sarah didn't say anything for a few moments. She just started to unload the supplies she had gathered for the men while she was in Cleveland. Then, as her anger and fear finally melted away, she asked the officer, "May I return to my home just outside of Cleveland then?"

"As long as you don't attempt to come back here, I don't care where you go."

CHAPTER 31
1863, CLEVELAND, TENNESSEE

S arah had been in her home only long enough to clean it well and put it in order before Ralph, Sam, and Elmer Pointer unexpectedly showed up at the farm. Sam had remembered from the hunting trip how to get there and had taken Elmer and Ralph along. Their work had ended when the Union army drove Bragg's army from their "unconquerable" position on the mountains overlooking Chattanooga. It had been a soldiers' battle, with the blue-clad soldiers outdoing what their commanding officers had ordered them to do. General Grant had been completely unprepared for the battle for Missionary Ridge. He had been confident that General Sherman could easily defeat the Confederate army under Bragg by attacking his northern flank. But the outnumbered men of the South had stalled his attack for most of the day of November 25, 1863. Late in the afternoon, General Thomas's men were ordered to attack uphill from the west and take the first of three Confederate defensive lines. They were ordered to occupy that line and then wait until the next morning to push their attack if it was needed. But when they had taken the first line, they hesitated only momentarily, then with great courage continued the uphill attack and took the next two lines, completely astonishing both blue and gray commanders. What surprised everyone even more was that it took only about an hour to complete the rout of Bragg's soldiers.

Sam was able to recount the events accurately because he was on the extended staff of General Grant and was present with the leaders during most of the day and witnessed the courageous men before, during, and after the battle.

Sarah then told Sam of her encounter with the Taylor brothers just after she had passed the message to Elmer about the transfer of Longstreet's corps. She was so disturbed that she did not have a reasonable response ready to tell her accusers. Had a few men had their way, she would not have survived the day.

"I am glad to be away from the fighting and don't think I want to do anymore spying," she said.

"We are not here to talk you into doing anything you don't want to do. We just thought that you would want to hear that your efforts were most helpful to the men and in a broader view of events will help to shorten the war. Had Thomas been forced to surrender Chattanooga, then the North would have needed to retake the same ground again. I have a letter from General Grant that he asked me to hand deliver to you."

Sarah took the letter and began to read the brief message. Sam watched her as she scanned it a second time and saw the blush that came to her face. "Are you all right? Has he said something that is embarrassing to you?" he asked.

"I'm not ashamed in any way, but he has been more than complimentary, and all I was doing was following your instructions the best I could." The note contained the general's gratitude for timely information that he claimed had saved men and boys from injury and death, at the risk of her own life.

Sarah reflected on those words over and over during the few days that Sam, Ralph, and Elmer were staying with her. Gradually, she realized that she could play a small part in shortening the war and more importantly, in so doing save a few lives, at the same risk as any other young person who wanted to do his or her part.

As the three young men were leaving, she said to them, "If you think that I can be helpful again anywhere in this war, you will be able to reach me in Pittsburgh at Ralph's home."

With that, the visit ended on a somber note for all four but especially for Sam as he realized how much he admired her courage and strength, especially after what she had recently been through. He had seen men face the horrible dangers of the battlefield mostly because they felt a powerful obligation to their friends and bond with their fellow soldiers. On the other hand, Sarah displayed the same determination, even though she had faced—and would continue to face—danger alone.

Before Sarah left for Pittsburgh, she wanted to make sure that Rebecca and Elizabeth understood that the lease with Chauncey's father had been broken because he had not paid any rent since the first of the year and had not occupied the farm. This meant that there was no one except her and her father who could allow the use of any property or livestock. She left them a paper stating that they could continue to occupy the small homes they lived in and use the land, farm equipment, and animals for their benefit.

Both husbands, Harry and Smitty, were still alive and well as far as their wives knew, and they both had hopes that the war would end soon and that the men would return safely home. Both were stationed in Savannah, Georgia, with the troops that were garrisoned there and had not seen much action—and that was just fine with their wives.

CHAPTER 32

1864, PITTSBURGH, PENNSYLVANIA

Sarah had arrived in Pittsburgh just after Christmas and found all of the Baxters at home. Ralph was on leave and would soon return to his duties with Sam, who was presently stationed in Chattanooga. Minnie had finished school and was volunteering at a local hospital that was caring for men from both armies who had lost limbs and were trying to retrain themselves so they would yet be useful in their lives. Mrs. Baxter had become very efficient in collecting the debts that were owed on her property so that her family was prospering during the war.

Matilda had stayed on with the Baxters, and Mrs. Baxter had insisted that she start to use her full name. "You speak so much better than most people I know, and you are very intelligent. I think it will always create a better impression if you use the more dignified name that the McFarlands gave you. The only better name would be if you could remember your childhood name from Africa."

Sarah and Matilda were talking one day about what had happened during the months they had been separated. "I had a troubling run-in with Amos Taylor. He wanted me arrested and made an example of for spying," Sarah started. "Do you remember the colonel that sent Marion Nelson home?"

"Yes, he seemed like he cared about her more than army regulations."

"There was a captain in charge of Amos and Clarence who talked the same way. He sent me home to Cleveland and told me not to come back. I was very relieved to get away with my wagon and mules," Sarah said. "You look tired, Matilda, and like something is the matter."

"I am tired but not from work. I have been thinking so much about my son, and I don't know how I will ever find him. Now I am also worried about Mrs. Baxter. She told me more about her first son who was taken from their front porch when he was two years old."

Sarah was shocked to hear this. She knew that there had been a son before Ralph but thought he had died of the fever. "What do you mean taken? I thought he died."

"One night, when I was feeling especially heartbroken, Mrs. Baxter told me more of the story. It happened when she was expecting Ralph Junior. She left his older brother, David, on the front porch for a few moments while she went into the house. When she came out, he was gone from the porch."

"Did he wander off?"

"She said that she and Ralph never found out. After their neighbors searched all over the area, a group from Ralph's work organized, and they searched for weeks but could never find a trace. Not clothing, not a toy doll he had been playing with, nothing, not his body. At one point, she prayed that they might at least know what had happened, even if he had died."

"How does she go on?" Sarah asked quietly.

"She said that if it hadn't been for the births of Ralph Junior and Minnie, she would have died. It helped me to know that she understood how much I want to find my son, Angus."

"But you still look tired and careworn."

"I don't think another person's pain is meant to take mine away. It just helps me know that she survives hers. And she goes on showing such love to others."

They talked quietly for a long time, waiting for Minnie to come home from her work and for Mrs. Baxter to return from visiting other widows.

The days before Christmas passed slowly while the country seemed to wait and watch to see what would happen the next year. Sarah was hoping that her father would come back to Pittsburgh for the holidays, but with the end of the year being so near, she did not have much hope of that happening.

She walked by Mrs. Baxter's room early on Christmas Eve and heard her quietly weeping. She tapped quietly on the door and asked if she could visit for a few moments.

"Yes, please come in," she replied quietly.

"Will you help me?" Sarah asked. "I have a troubled conscience."

Mrs. Baxter looked shocked. "What could possibly be hurting you so much that you need to talk?"

"I feel like I have betrayed myself and the young men and boys I wanted to help when I first left Knoxville. I gave vital information to Elmer, and so to General Grant, about Confederate troop movements around Chattanooga. I have worried ever since that men have died because of the information I gave."

"Sarah, men are dying now because of the many like Matilda who have been dying for over two hundred years. Your father believes that we are paying for that blood with this terrible war. My Ralph said that your father knew slavery was wrong and gave up his part of any inheritance because he felt like the sin would destroy him. Do you feel bad about helping Matilda?"

"No. In fact, after the captain told Amos and Clarence to let me go, I overheard them saying that I cheated them out of their slave. It gives me satisfaction to think that I didn't ever pay them, but instead, helped her get here."

While she was in Pittsburgh Sarah received a letter a few weeks after Christmas announcing that Sam had been promoted to the field rank of colonel and was being reassigned to the Army of the Potomac. He asked her if she would be willing to go to Richmond to work with the Southern army as a nurse and to help with the transfer of information through a network of agents working there.

This sounded like a safer way to serve than as an active spy with the army, and as she thought about the idea, she decided on her own that if she were working with injured men, she might be able to encourage them to leave the army and just go home. She did not realize how dimly Southerners would view one who was encouraging desertion.

One evening in early February, while at the dinner table, she was talking with Matilda, Mrs. Baxter, and Minnie about Sam's proposal to go to Richmond.

"Why would he want you to leave here where we are all safe and happy?" Mrs. Baxter asked. "You have had danger and adventure enough."

"I told him, Elmer, and Ralph that if they thought I could do anything to help shorten the war, I would do it. I could also try to talk wounded Confederate soldiers into going home to stay. That might even save a life or two."

"I was hoping that you would stay here and continue to help Matilda and me in our volunteer work," Minnie added.

The conversation went on for some time, but it left Sarah more determined to go to Washington later in the month.

As she thought more and more about the proposal, Sarah came up with a different way to convey information to Sam through the Northern agents. She thought that instead of any direct contact, she could try to encode the information in her drawings. Then she hoped that an arranged pick-up place could be used to make the actual transfer. If she could figure out a way to give Sam numbers and figures by using sketches, it would give him accurate information, and it might be safer than the normal channels of written messages or face-to-face reports.

She knew it would take some refinement of thought and that she would need to prepare one booklet for Sam and one for herself. She began work immediately and found a special release from tension in sketching, which was both something she loved and something that occupied a lot of time.

The most obvious encryption would be to hide letters and numbers in the lines of the drawings, but she would need a certain signal to let Sam know what each drawing meant and contained. It would be a good idea to send multiple pictures to confuse anyone who might intercept the sketches. The more she thought about the idea, the more excited she became and wanted to go to Richmond to help end the war as soon as possible.

She spent most of the month of February preparing for Sam a small booklet of the codes she would use in the sketches. She also drew a number of sketches that could be used as decoy pictures and to show Sam what a picture without any useful information looked like. She devised a way to let him know where the different corps were stationed and their strength. She had no idea what she was doing, but the effort made her feel a lot better about herself and the contribution she could make.

Sam, for his part, had been spending the month of February in Washington trying to make some sense out of the different spy rings that were operating in and around Richmond. The quality of information they were able to generate depended to a great extent on their own understanding of what was needed and then how to make a timely transfer of that information. Often, the newspapers had more information and were delivered more quickly than agents could get their reports through the lines of the military.

Sam decided that he needed one person in Richmond to coordinate all of the efforts of the people involved. The problem would be to get someone whom the authorities in Richmond would not recognize as a threat. Naturally this person and any compromised agents risked death if they were discovered—and that was a risk anyone taking on the responsibility would have to be aware of and still be willing to take.

Sam had considered all of his options and approached his commanding officer about the possibility of serving out the war in Richmond himself. He tried to persuade General Boynton that he would be the best candidate for the responsibility because of his already having organized some of the people who were on site in the Confederate capital. With one or two exceptions, they were lifelong residents and had a thorough knowledge of the city and the country surrounding it. They also had some knowledge of the way the army was being supplied and reinforced. Sam said that he could gather the information daily or weekly and then forward it to the Union army via courier.

General Boynton was adamant that it would be unwise to have his direct subordinate, the man who was most familiar with the working of both sides of the spy system, away in Richmond when he would likely be needed nearer the Union capital and telegraph that connected to the main army. He also pointed out that both Confederate lines and Union lines could not possibly be drawn tightly enough to prohibit a skillful courier from travelling between the two armies. A single person, who looked on the surface like an innocent traveler, would have a much better chance of passing through the lines and delivering the necessary intelligence. Sam could then pass it along to the appropriate field commanders. The telegraph system that the Union army employed was centered in Washington and had the added value of transmitting information quickly around most of the Union-controlled territory. The end of the discussion came when General Boynton instructed Sam to find the best people on site in

Richmond and instruct them carefully on passing along any useful information in a carefully prearranged code.

Sam considered all of the people who had agreed to give information and found that he trusted Elmer Pointer to carry on the work of espionage more discreetly than anyone else that he had yet recruited. Elmer would place himself in Richmond at the earliest possible date.

CHAPTER 33

1864, WASHINGTON, DC

Sarah left for Washington the last week of February and arrived around the first of March. It took her a full day to track down where Sam worked, and then she had to make an appointment to see him. He was delighted that she had accepted the idea of going to Richmond, and he was even more delighted with her work on the drawings and the booklet he'd need to interpret them. However, he explained to her that he would not be in a place where he could take the information directly. She would give the coded drawings to Elmer, and he would transfer the information to Sam, who would immediately telegraph the details to General Grant's staff.

Sarah was surprised because she had been so preoccupied with her work in Pittsburgh that she did not realize that General Grant had been promoted to the rank of lieutenant general in the Union army and now outranked all officers in the regular army. He had also decided to stay with the Army of the Potomac so that he could avoid the politics in Washington. Grant had been one of the commanders who listened to and used information given by both civilian and military spies.

"It sounds like a roundabout way to get information to the army," Sarah said.

"It is a little cumbersome, but it is about as good as we can do. The telegraph makes it possible. There is a special unit with the army whose sole responsibility is to string telegraph wire and make sure that wherever the army commander is that he will have quick access to a telegraph operator so that he can communicate quickly with Washington," Sam explained.

"I have taken the liberty of inviting one other person to this meeting that I believe will be important to the success of the whole operation," Sam continued. "He should have been here by now. but I can tell you that I have asked your father to be part of our unit. It will give you a natural cover if you and he go to Richmond together. He'll be posing as a wounded soldier from Tennessee who is now unable to fight, and you will be his faithful daughter who wants to care for him and other wounded men. Since the Union now controls most of Tennessee, including the area where your farm is, you want to be in Richmond, where you can help your cause the most. What do you think?"

For a few moments, Sarah looked at Sam in complete wonder and amazement. She was almost speechless that the planning had gone so far as to consider having both her and her father spy for the North. It made her wonder who else would be brought into the plan.

There was a knock on the door, and Sam's secretary, Corporal William Lewis, poked his head in and said that General Boynton needed to talk with Sam immediately. Sam excused himself before he received Sarah's answer to his question. She was relieved because it gave her a chance to overcome her surprise at the plan he had proposed and to try to consider it calmly, to figure out how it would change her own involvement. When Sam finally reentered the office, she was quite composed—until she saw that he had both her father and Elmer with him.

Sarah had grown fond of Elmer during the short visit that he and Sam had made to her home after the fighting at Chattanooga. It was then she realized that there were men she had met that made her infatuation with Chauncey seem very immature. She blushed slightly when the men came into the office, but they attributed it to be her excitement at seeing her father up and around and looking much better than the last time she had seen him.

"I am sure that the two of you have a lot you would like to discuss without Elmer and me present. Elmer has been in Richmond for just over a week and is negotiating a lease for a stable and blacksmith shop. He will be the main contact and will gather any information that you provide, along with reports from other Union sympathizers. He will be in charge of making sure that all of the agents are safe, and if there is any kind of breakdown of secrecy, he'll make sure the whole network is shut down and everyone connected evacuated as cleanly as possible. Please take a couple of days to decide how far you want to go with this mission—and to decide if you are all right working together, as I have explained."

Sarah and her father then left the office and went to a nearby boarding house where they were shown to the rooms that Sam had arranged for them while they were in Washington.

"Mrs. Baxter told me that you only stayed in Pittsburgh a little while after I left for home," Sarah said.

Ted said "I felt like I was in the way of those three women wanting to do me good. I felt a little confined, so I returned to my unit who were then in Washington."

"I was hoping that you would come back to Pittsburgh during the holidays. Were you afraid of more attention?" Sarah asked.

"No, but I felt like I had spent more time away than most men with similar injuries and felt obligated to be present so someone else could take leave. I was interested when I heard that you were compelled to leave the Southern army so soon. It seems to me that you have been uniquely lucky during the time you have spent away from home and family," Sarah's father said. "To think that you carry a wound from one incident and a memory of extreme danger from another. Either should have taught you a little more caution about accepting another request to go into harm's way."

Sarah thought for a moment and realized that she had been preparing to talk to her father about Marion almost since the time she had been at Chancellorsville. "When I first went along with Chauncey, I had no idea of the filth and boredom that was the normal daily life of a man in the army," she started. "I had some romantic idea that there was continual fighting, and that only the unattractive or cowardly or craven were killed or injured. Those whose lives would not matter anyway were the ones who were required to pay the price of war. Then, I met a girl who had been in the fighting in Virginia. She and the boy she loved had traveled from Georgia to Virginia, been married, and then she was widowed at Fredericksburg. When I met her, she was still hiding her real identity and age—and the fact that she was pregnant. When it was certain that there would be a spring offensive and that the Union army, led by General Hooker, would attack, she confided in me because she wanted someone to reach her parents if she were killed. Of all of the people I have seen in the armies, she was the bravest. She wasn't fighting for the Union or the Confederates but because she loved her butternut-clad boy-husband. She thought he would want her to continue to fight because they had started together. She was with Stonewall Jackson's corps during Chancellorsville, and it was said of her that she kept up with the men and fought bravely in spite of her condition. I believe that it's her example more than anything else that gives me the will to be of some use to you and anyone else whose life has been affected by this war."

Ted had never heard Sarah give a speech before, and he was impressed by her explanation and her thoughtful reasoning. More than that, as he thought of what she must have gone through during the past year, tears of love and admiration ran down his cheeks as he compared his daughter to the other woman he had loved during his life. He realized that she was far more like her mother in spirit than he had ever before realized. She was maturing before his eyes because of the independent decisions she had made during the past year. She had been exposed to war and injury, death and heartbreak in ways she would have never experienced in Cleveland or Knoxville or Pittsburgh. The part that he admired more than he thought possible was her determination to do something good and worthwhile, despite realizing that the consequences could be deadly.

"Have you changed so completely from your stance before the war that the South should be able to leave the Union without being coerced to remain? Do you now feel that you will be risking your life for something that is good?" he asked.

"I have thought long and hard about giving information to the Union about what was happening in the Confederate army that was threatening Grant's army in Chattanooga. Was I right or wrong? Was it good or traitorous? There are men and boys who are fighting for the South whom I love as I would my own brothers, and I don't want to see them damaged. Even so, like you I have come to realize that slaves have bled physically, spiritually, and emotionally more than the wounded in both armies. They deserve a chance to live without someone owning them and controlling their agency. I hope I can do this with their freedom in mind and perhaps stop feeling guilty for my earlier, ignorant stance about slavery and how 'well' some were treated."

Ted thought about this. "I think we are both ready now to go to Richmond. I don't think there is a lot we can do for the Union army there, but if we can help some Rebel soldiers accept the fact that the war is lost or that their families need them at home, maybe that will be enough."

It was a lot more complicated than either Ted or Sarah anticipated. Beyond the complex matter of getting them into a position where they could enter Richmond without suspicion, they would need to be given stories that would not be easy to verify but would at the same time seem very plausible.

CHAPTER 34
1864, RICHMOND, VIRGINIA

The initial push by the Union army began in the late spring of 1864. The Army of the Potomac started to push into the area of woods known as the Wilderness, west of Chancellorsville, while the Union army of Tennessee began their march toward Atlanta. The strategy was to make sure that neither large Confederate army would be able to give any support to the other.

The fighting in the Wilderness was bloody and without vision, like two heavyweight boxers blinded with sweat and blood, each punching at his opponent without knowing exactly where his head was located. It took almost as long as the 1863 fight around Chancellorsville, but the difference, after horrendous casualties to both armies, was that the Union army moved south instead of retreating north to lick its wounds and wait for General Lee to outflank them again.

Sarah started to see the overwhelming consequences before the battle was even over. There was a huge influx of severely wounded boys brought to the hospital from the Army of Northern Virginia. More than at any other battle she had witnessed, she felt the heart-breaking wrench twisting her inside as she saw what war could really do to the body of a healthy man in the physical prime of life. She sat by many fatally injured boys in their last hours of earthly pain, calling for their mothers. She realized that there was something private and sacred about these last moments in their lives, and that it was appropriate that they would want their mothers close to comfort them and lead them beyond the veil into the unknown.

After two weeks of witnessing this utterly senseless waste, she was ready to curse the generals of all of the armies for the slaughter, and the politicians who were not bleeding but sitting safely in their protected offices, thinking that they could solve the country's problems with wordy laws and regulations. She decided to talk the person she worked for whom she trusted, Olivia Landeach, who had been working in the hospital since the casualties started coming in from the battle of First Manassas. She had been a witness to the increasing number of wounded men and boys as the war progressed, an increase triggered by the use of more sophisticated weapons and the greater numbers of men involved. Mrs. Landeach had grown discouraged, much the same as Sarah, but she had been able to cope with her feelings because of something she read in the Bible: "He riseth from supper and laid aside his garments; and took a towel and girded himself. After that he poureth water into a basin and began to wash the disciples' feet, and to wipe them with the towel wherewith he was girded."

After reading this, Mrs. Landeach started to return to the hospital after her evening meal. She would get a basin of warm water and a towel and go to those who seemed most in need and gently wash and dry their feet.

When Sarah approached her, she asked, "Why do you wash their feet? Why not their wounds?"

In answer, Mrs. Landeach had her sit down and remove her shoes and stockings. Sarah was overly tired at the time and realized that she had never had such a warm and loving feeling as having her tired, sore feet gently washed with warm water and carefully dried by someone else.

When she left Richmond that night to take some boys home to their families to finish their recovery, she forgot to leave a note for her father.

"Elmer, I have come to find out if you have heard anything from Sarah," Ted asked. "She has not returned home since she left the hospital yesterday, and I am worried about where she is."

"She must have come here last night because her mules were gone this morning when I came in. She told me a couple of days ago that she was worried about them because they had not had good feed for weeks. I was not around, but I can't think that anyone else could have taken them," Elmer replied. "Maybe she thought she could take them to a place where they could be better cared for."

Ted thought about that for a moment. "I think she would be worried that no matter where she could take them that one of the armies would requisition them and use them to pull wagons or cannons. She is more sensitive about the safety of those animals than about many of the men she takes care of." Then, as he thought more about what he had said, he added, "However, these last few weeks she has been showing more and more stress because of the untold number of wounded that have been arriving. It seems like both General Lee and General Grant have lost their ability to maneuver their armies, and because of that, the battles seem to be even bloodier."

"Has she given you any useful information during the past month?" Ted then asked Elmer.

"Her rate of reporting has remained steady the whole time the two of you have been in Richmond," Elmer replied. "Her sense of what is important and the way she uses illustrations to mask her news are unique. I believe her code will be impossible to detect by anyone who may accidently gain a view of her submissions. I wish all of the information given to me was as carefully prepared. I guess what I am trying to say is that no one should be able to recognize that she is giving needed intelligence to the Northern armies."

"I am not as worried about that as I am about her starting to encourage boys to just give up the fight and go home. I think she feels that she can save more lives by doing that than anything else, but it could be far more dangerous because of the number of people who know about it," said her worried father.

"I have tried to talk to her about being discreet when she approaches anyone, and she told me she never comes out and says that they should go home. She just encourages them to talk about home and their families as much as possible. By doing that, she is hoping to increase their desire to both live and return their homes. If that is all she is doing, I don't see how anyone can accuse her of trying to incite desertion."

"I hope you're right, Elmer. She is living a life that I would have never chosen for myself, let alone my only child. I worry that she is becoming so emotionally involved with the wounded that she may make a decision that she will regret."

"Do you worry that she will decide to marry one of the wounded just out of extreme sympathy?"

"The thought has crossed my mind and, obviously, yours too."

"Every so often I ask her if she is attracted to any of the men in her care, especially those she mentions more than once. She says that she hasn't met anyone who makes her feel anything like what she thought she felt for Chauncey last year. Do you know why she would refer to him in the past tense?"

"I don't know, but I think as she got to know him better, she realized she could not trust him because of the way he treated his recruits. The one thing she did tell me was that the sergeants who were with him and the men whom he recruited did not respect him. For her, that would be the end of any romantic ideas she had for anyone."

CHAPTER 35

1864, ON THE ROAD TO TEMPORARY, VIRGINIA

Sarah made a quick decision to leave Richmond. The only person who knew about her leaving, besides the wounded soldiers she took with her, was the matron, Olivia Landeach, who was in charge of the men she was taking. Mrs. Landeach asked her if she could help get three hopelessly wounded men to their homes in the western part of the state. Sarah told her she would be happy to help in any way she could. She also explained that she had boarded two mules and her wagon at a livery stable and that she could transport the men in the wagon. She also asked Mrs. Landeach to let her father know where she had gone if he came looking for her.

Mrs. Landeach cautioned Sarah to be extremely careful while traveling because the patrols of both Confederate and Union cavalry seemed to be freely ranging throughout northwestern Virginia. They could be trusted for the most part, but if she ran into deserters, she could place herself and her charges in real danger. "Please try to stay in a village or at a farm if you need to stop overnight.

Usually, if there are other women around, they can warn you of any danger and help provide food and comfort for these boys you are taking home."

The trip would require about three days' travel to a village called Temporary, no more than a tavern, four or five farms, and a couple of good-sized old plantations. There were taverns and inns along the way so Sarah thought she would be perfectly safe, especially while traveling with the three young men. She was given Confederate money in abundance to cover expenses so that she felt that she would not need to reveal her cache of gold coins.

Typical of young people, she did not want to get permission from her father or clear it with Elmer before she left. She felt confident after all of her travel and luck up to this point that nothing could happen that would be more dangerous than what she had already faced. She obviously did not understand the desperate nature of some men who had left the army and were hiding in the hills and mountains west of Richmond.

On the third day of travel, they approached an old, apparently deserted plantation that looked like it might have water and possibly be a good place to rest the mules and give them a chance to graze. As they approached the mansion, a man stepped out on to the large front veranda. He was dressed in the remnants of a fine suit of clothes that had seen much better days.

"What's your business here?" the figure asked in a sweet-sounding Southern drawl.

Sarah had to take a closer look and realized that she had again been fooled by a woman dressed in men's clothes. There was an old woman buried beneath the old felt cap and oversized ragged clothing.

"I have three young men who have been in hospital at Richmond and are returning home. They have each lost a leg and are unable to fight in the war anymore," Sarah answered. "We were hoping to let the mules graze and get some fresh water. Do you have a well?"

"There's a well in the back of the house by the kitchen, and you can let the mules roam and find whatever they can." The old woman then asked the men, "Are you able to come inside?"

As the men climbed slowly from the wagon, Sarah began to unhitch the mules. When they were free, a man stepped from the side of the porch and leveled a shotgun at her. "Just let the mules go, and you step inside with the men." Sarah couldn't imagine what was going on but dutifully followed his instructions.

"Now, young woman, what are you doing with these three criminals?" the old woman asked.

"What do you mean, criminals? They have served their cause and given their all to the Confederacy," Sarah responded.

"The Confederacy," the old lady spat. "They started this war and then bought our horses and mules using their worthless money. We have not been able to put in a crop that would sustain us since the first of 1863. Now, it's obvious that they will lose the war, and they are still fighting. That means to me that anyone still fighting for them is a criminal."

Sarah could not believe what she was hearing. She looked at the young men she was transporting and realized that she felt a strong obligation to protect them against this woman and her belligerent companion.

Suddenly, one of the men, Joseph Davis, spoke up. "Wait a minute. You don't belong on this farm. You're that old crazy Henrietta Owens who owns the tavern just a piece this side of Temporary. You were one of the people who insisted that we should whip the Yankees and send them to the hell they deserved. I joined the army when I was still sixteen because of people like you. What are you doing here?"

Having been unmasked, the old woman hesitated and then said that the tavern had been burned down by a small unit of Confederate infantry who had heard that she had been trading home-brew whiskey and other supplies to the Yankees because they would pay her in Yankee money. After that, she came to this abandoned farm and tried to eke out an existence. Her nephew hunted in the surrounding hills, and they had a small kitchen garden in which they were able to raise barely enough vegetables to survive.

Her nephew had been in the Confederate army until the battle of First Manassas when he was so frightened that he had skedaddled in all the confusion. He was now holding a steady aim on the group of three young men, all of whom were all handicapped physically and not carrying any weapons, except Joseph, who was carrying a bowie knife.

Sarah spoke up. "There isn't any reason that you need to point that gun at the men. They are harmless. I'm taking them to their home in Temporary and then returning to the hospital in Richmond. We won't trouble you anymore." With that, she started for the door but was brought up suddenly by the roar of the shotgun.

She turned quickly to see the youngest of her charges fall to the ground, bleeding from his good leg.

"The next shot will end his life," Henrietta said. "Before you leave, I will make a careful search of your wagon. You must be carrying something that we can use. You can help me, missy." She told her nephew to kill the men if they moved and then took Sarah by the arm and guided her out the door.

"They need to help Henry and make sure that the bleeding is stopped," Sarah said.

"But that's all," the old woman said. "Anything else and he will kill Henry. I don't think he ever liked him anyway."

Sarah was worried that the old woman might be curious enough that she would find the hidden cache of gold coins. She never carried all of the money her father had given her, but she always had enough that she could get out of a tight spot. She wondered if this situation warranted letting some of the money go to save the young men. But then, she couldn't be sure that even if she gave up the cash, any of them would survive.

She decided. As they neared the wagon, she said, "I have a few gold coins in a compartment under the seat. It is hard to find, but I can show you."

"Are you pulling my leg? I haven't seen real gold coins, not since the war started. I don't believe you would be foolish enough to carry them with you."

"I have them. Look here under these boards. All you need to do is slide them out, and you will see the compartment."

Henrietta carefully watched the girl and then removed the boards. In the compartment was a small sack that clinked as she picked it up. Her attention was completely riveted on opening the bag while Sarah picked up the large cavalry revolver Ralph gave her before she went to Chattanooga. She quickly pushed Henrietta's hat over her eyes, grabbed a fistful of hair at the back of her head, and twisted. Henrietta cried out in pain, but by then, it was too late. Sarah had the gun pointed at the base of her skull and said, "Be quiet. We are going to walk calmly up to the door. If you want to live, you had better get your nephew to give one of the men his shotgun."

They made their way up the porch, and Henrietta tried to use the doorframe for leverage to push Sarah off, but she was not nearly as strong as the grip the young woman had on her hair. She cried out in pain again, and her nephew quickly turned to see what was going on—his first mistake. He wheeled back to aim the gun at one of the men, but he was too late. By then, a crippled young soldier pushed the gun back toward the door as it went off. For the third time, Henrietta cried out in pain as the pellets from the shotgun slammed into her left shoulder. In the same instant, Sarah fired a shot that could not have found its mark better if she had had time to aim. The 44-caliber Colt bullet found a target in the heart of the young nephew. Sarah was so shocked by the result of her action that she froze, completely horrified and speechless.

Fortunately, Joseph Davis, who knew a killing shot when he saw one, grabbed the shotgun and quickly took control of the situation.

There was now one dead man and two injured people. He quickly prompted Sarah to start thinking about what needed to be done to help both people. "Let's get these two bandaged enough to get them to Temporary. It's still a good half-day journey," he said.

With that, Sarah was able to gather her thoughts. First, she attended to the young soldier, Henry Stuart, tying a clean cloth from her wagon tightly around the wound in his leg. She knew it would be painful for him to ride and be jostled in the wagon, but there was nothing she could do about that. Henrietta was another matter. She was unconscious and probably wasn't feeling much at the moment. After Sarah had done the best she could to bandage the injured pair, she went out to get the mules hitched back up. She recovered the bag of coins from Henrietta, hid them again, and then helped everyone into the wagon.

CHAPTER 36

1864, TEMPORARY, VIRGINIA

After they had been on the road for a couple of hours, Joseph pointed to a partially burned, rundown shack. "That is what Henrietta calls her tavern."

It was not badly burned, but it looked completely abandoned. "I think she must have been lying to us about 'criminals' burning it down," Sarah said.

"We have about an hour to go before we reach Henry's place on this side of town. I believe you will like his family. They are the kindest people I know and will help us in any way they can," Joseph said.

As they approached the farm, Sarah was astonished to see in the pasture a mule that her father had sold about two years before the war started. She pointed it out to Joseph, and he said to her, "How can you be sure that mule came from your farm?"

"It was one of my favorite young mules. If Henry's parents are as kind as you say, then that mule would fit right in with their household. It was one of the most even-tempered animals we ever raised."

When they arrived at the front door of the Stuart home, Sarah recognized the man who greeted them. "I remember you from when you bought a mule from my father," she said. "I am Sarah Clarke, and I saw you at our farm when you picked up the mule."

"So you're that young girl whose father said she knew more about his animals than he did. I remember. Now I have a question for you. Do you really remember me, or do you remember that mule and know me from that memory?"

Sarah blushed at the question because the truth was that she naturally had a better memory of a mule that she raised than the man she had known for only a day. "I saw the mule in the field and knew that it was one that we sold. Then it dawned on me who the buyer was. I'm glad to see that he is on a farm and not pulling a caisson or cannon."

"We don't take him away from the farm, and whenever we hear of any army patrols in the area, we keep him well hidden," Mr. Stuart said. "I see you have brought my son home along with some of his friends. You are all welcome to come in for the night and rest. We don't have a lot, but what food we do have is meant to be shared by our guests."

With that statement, Henry spoke up. "Father, I've been wounded by this woman's nephew." He pointed at Henrietta. "He shot me in the leg with a shotgun."

At that, Mr. Stuart looked more closely at those in the wagon and recognized the old woman still dressed in ragged men's clothing.

"I heard that her tavern was abandoned after people found out she was collaborating with some thieves who live in the back country. Where were you when you were shot, and where is her nephew?"

Joseph spoke up then. "This young woman will need to tell you the whole story, but can we bring Henry into the house and maybe even this woman? She was also shot by her nephew, just as he was being killed by Miss Sarah."

Everyone was able to make it into the large farmhouse. The wounded were cleaned up, bandaged with fresh, clean, cotton cloths, and placed in comfortable rooms. Even Mrs. Owens was shown consideration in spite of her obviously bad character. Then, Mrs. Stuart served a meal that was not overly generous but nourishing and tasty.

The after-dinner conversation centered around the Wilderness battle in which all three young men had been wounded and the fact that the Yankee army had not retreated, even though they suffered more casualties than the Confederates.

Sarah spoke up. "Their new commander, General Grant, came from the west, and he was the one responsible for the victories in Tennessee and Mississippi. The rumor is that he won't retreat without being soundly beaten."

"I don't think we have enough men then to make him retreat," Mr. Stuart said. "I believe, if you are right about his character, Jefferson Davis should start looking for an honorable peace settlement. Otherwise we will lose even more of our young men to serious injury and death for no good reason."

Mr. Stuart's family was surprised at this discouraged-sounding statement. They had always looked to him for optimism. In fact, there had been many times in the past few years that he had been overly positive about the successful outcome of the war. Now with two of his three sons still serving in the Rebel army, and Henry wounded and obviously hurting from the shotgun blast, it seemed that he would like to give up and do whatever Abe Lincoln wanted.

With that unhappy thought, the rest of Sarah's party decided to move on toward the farm where Joseph lived, about an hour away.

When they arrived, they told of their experience at the old plantation house, the death of Henrietta's nephew, and the wounding of her and Henry. Sarah was so exhausted that when she was given an uncomfortable couch to sleep on, she fell into a dreamless sleep and didn't wake until late afternoon the next day. When she did wake, she was disoriented for a few minutes, wondering where she was.

When she started to remember the events of the past day, she started to quietly weep at the thought of having shot and killed the young man. Suddenly, the door opened, and Joseph's mother, Ruth, came through the open door and sat down next to Sarah on the couch.

"Please tell me what brings a young woman like you on this kind of a journey. I talked to Joseph this morning, and he said that you were one of the most caring nurse attendants at the hospital in Richmond and that you were particular about how their wounds should be properly cleaned and dressed. Now I find you weeping for who knows what reason."

Sarah was astonished that Joseph's mother did not understand why she felt so dirty inside. "I have seen more mutilation and death in this war than I ever imagined could exist. And now I cannot comprehend the death of that young man at my hand. He must be about the same age as Joseph."

Ruth looked at her for a minute. "He is the same physical age, but Joseph has always been older in his mind. Jeremiah Owens was too influenced by Henrietta and her worthless late husband. They have always lived a shade too close to dishonest practices, all the way from watering down whiskey to telling a lie just because it sounded good at the time. No one who knew them well would ever do business with them and that nephew who was even more dishonest and mean."

"I still cannot justify the reckless shot that I fired at him. It seemed to happen so fast that I had no control over any part of the event."

"You have returned my son safely to me, and I will not fault the way you accomplished that. But now you should be concerned about returning to Richmond on your own. Why don't you stay with us a little longer until you can make a good plan to return? Maybe you could find some trustworthy traveling companions."

Sarah thought about this. "I would like to at least catch my breath and rest a little more. My mules could use a couple of days of good grazing, and if there is any grain in the area, maybe I could buy some for them."

Ruth paused for a moment. "Sarah, I think you should worry a little more about your own health than whether those mules have grain. You rest and let my husband, Fred, worry about your mules. He can get them in shape for any travel, while you make up your mind to feel better inside."

Sarah then thought that Ruth must have read her mind about the guilt she was feeling.

She spent the next few days in another home where the parents and children shared confidence and harmony. It seemed very much like the Baxter home in Pittsburgh except for the soft Southern drawl that Sarah was so fond of hearing. She was able to gain a little relief from the shocking turn of events at the old plantation and could at least begin to cope with her own feelings. The experience made her want to talk with her father though and let him know where she was staying and that she was all right. Even as she had these thoughts, she realized that it would be impossible to see him until she returned to Richmond. This was the principal reason that she insisted on leaving a few days later.

CHAPTER 37

1864, THE LONG ROAD HOME

The morning before she left, Fred Davis pointed out that the safest way to return would be to travel northwest along the road to Bedford, where she would have a chance to pick up a train to Richmond.

The next morning, Sarah took her leave and took the rough road toward Bedford. Along the way, she started to become more and more despondent and then angry about the events that had occurred since she had arrived in Richmond. Normally, she was not one to feel sorry for herself but having witnessed the death and destruction of the war, and then having it touch her so personally when she shot and killed a young man, she became depressed. At length, she became so agitated that she whipped the mules and made them run for too long a time. She felt her team and wagon starting to lose control as she hit a very rough part in the road, and she labored to maintain her seat on the wagon. The mules were as close to being out of control as she had ever seen them, and she feared that they would now run away.

With the greatest difficulty, she regained her seat and then applied the wagon brake and pulled back on the reins as hard as she could. It took some anxious moments for the mules to stop with the wagon, and when they did, they registered their fear with their snorting and braying. Sarah climbed down from the wagon, took the reins, and started to walk the mules to cool them down and give herself time to think about what she had just done.

She started to imagine that she was having a conversation with her father. In her mind, she told him why she was so troubled. Then, very quietly in her mind, she heard his voice repeat something she had heard him say when she was a lot younger, still learning about training the mules. "Is it good for you to be angry?" he would say. Then he would calmly repeat to her what her anger could accomplish if she changed it to solving a problem rather than letting it eat at her and turn destructive. She thought more and more about her situation and about how Henrietta and her nephew tried to waylay her group when they were at their weakest. She came to picture them not as less than human, but as people that she could first pity and then forgive. Then the hardest thought came to her when she realized that a great deal of her pent-up anger was directed toward Chauncey, for the brutal way that he had murdered Marty.

How could she ever not be angry with him? He had not knowingly hurt her, but he had destroyed someone that she loved as a younger brother. It was easier for her to let go of what people had deliberately done to hurt her, but this was different because of what he had done to another person.

After walking on foot for more than an hour, she knew that the mules were now cool enough that they could easily be retired for the night. She was exhausted from both her physical exertions and the mental anguish she was suffering. She started to look for a place to make a good open-air camp. She stopped the wagon and tied off the mules so that they would not wander while she looked carefully for a place that would offer as much safety as possible and still provide a little area where she could allow the animals to graze and rest.

Sarah had a fitful sleep that night, going over and over in her mind the events of the past week and the horrible scene at Gettysburg. While she was no longer as angry, she could not forget Chauncey's betrayal and the seeming uncontrollable shooting of the young man at the plantation. She finally fell into a deeper sleep toward early morning and was awakened by a profound dream she had of her father. He had never been one to preach to her, but in this dream, he was clearly preaching a sermon that would have a lasting effect on Sarah's peace of mind. All she could remember of his sermon was a statement that she clung to long enough to write it on one of the blank sheets that she had with her in her drawing papers. He said, "You must learn to have the patience to allow an all-knowing Savior to balance the scales of mercy and justice between all people, especially whenever the circumstances touch your own life."

She contemplated that statement during the rest of the trip back to Richmond and tried to work out what it would take to gain that patience. What she did know was that the thought of her father saying it to her in her dream was already bringing her troubled spirit peace enough to face the next hour and the next day.

She would need all of the relief she could gather to continue to pursue the double life she was living. In those early weeks of spring, the war was continuing at an intensity that had not been known since it began. In spite of horrendous casualties on both sides, neither General Lee nor General Grant felt that he was in a position to end the fighting. General Lee, because of his responsibility to protect the Confederate capital, was unable to maneuver with the boldness he had shown in splitting his army to gain key victories the first three summers of the war. General Grant had shown the same kind of aggressive tactics when he was fighting his way to lay siege to Vicksburg the summer before. But now he knew he was locked in conflict with someone just as aggressive as himself, and at an instinctive level, he was determined to continue the fight to push the Rebel army back to Richmond.

The pressure that this kind of fighting put on the medical facilities of the South broke many people down. Especially affected were those who were trying to help the injured regain enough strength so that they could be sent back into the fighting.

Sarah's goal as an agent for the Union was in direct conflict with the South's ultimate goal for those lightly wounded young soldiers. She would, in any subtle way she could, remind them of their loved ones at home and how desperately they were needed back on their farms and in their villages. She wanted to save any Southern boy she could by having him leave the fighting. She felt for every Southern life that was saved, a Northern boy would also be able to return home from the war when the fighting was finally over.

She was also upset that the leaders of the South kept feeling that they would be able to hold out long enough to make the Northern population change their goal of winning the war on the battlefield. In Pittsburgh, she had seen firsthand the industrial capacity of the North and sensed the resolve in families like the Baxters. She knew instinctively that they would ultimately not give up. She had heard talk of the hope that Abraham Lincoln would not be reelected and that a new president would be willing to treat for peace at any price. She thought that people in the North had already committed to paying an even higher price for freedom than the Southern people could match, and so the hopes of leaders in the South were groundless.

CHAPTER 38
1864, RICHMOND, VIRGINIA

The hard fighting toward Richmond continued through the middle of June, when the Union commander decided to stop his aggressive attack campaign and started to lay siege at Petersburg and Richmond. The casualties on both sides had been very heavy, and the hospital where Sarah was helping was filled to more than its capacity with suffering men and boys. However, now that Sarah had become more accustomed to the numbers and had found a way to cope emotionally, she filled her days with doing as much good as she could to help the wounded.

During one particularly long day at the beginning of July, she was helping a wounded soldier by starting to cut away his tunic from the left shoulder. "Be careful what you expose, Sarah. I don't want to be immodest in front of all these men." Sarah looked closely at the dirty face that was attached to the voice and recognized Marion.

Her questions flooded out all in a single sentence. "What are you doing here? How long have you been in Richmond? Where is your baby? Did you have a son or daughter? Where is your baby?" she repeated.

Marion looked at Sarah and said, "I'll answer all of your questions if you will get me out of this hospital. I don't think that I am badly injured, but I don't want to be with all these men," she whispered.

Sarah thought for a few moments and realized that she had barely enough space in her room at the boarding house for herself and her father, but she would ask him if he would mind bunking with Elmer or any of the friends he had made while he was in Richmond.

"I'll take you to the boarding house where I am staying. I believe we can make room for one more guest. But please tell me about your baby." Sarah was now talking in a low whisper so that the other soldiers around them wouldn't hear.

She helped Marion to her feet and started her moving toward the door of the ward they were in when Mrs. Landeach confronted them, asking what they were doing. Sarah gently took her by the arm and nodded to the door with eyes that begged the woman to come with them.

When they were outside the ward, Sarah whispered, "This is my friend Marion Nelson, and she has been wounded. She asked me to take her out of the ward full of men, and so I want to take her to my boarding house to take care of her."

Olivia Landeach tried to respond, but she was so taken aback by this incomprehensible situation that all she could do was nod slowly. Finally, she said, "Let me help you get her to your home. I think you are right that she will have a better chance of recovering there."

When they arrived at Sarah's room in the boarding house, they were able to help Marion remove her tunic. They saw that the bullet had gone cleanly through the muscle above her collarbone so the wound, though very painful, was not serious, unless infection set in. Sarah felt that she knew how to prevent that from the advice she had received from Terrance so long ago.

Mrs. Landeach excused herself to return to the hospital and told Sarah that she thought that she should stay with Marion until she was sure she was comfortable and would feel safe. "And don't wear her out by asking too many questions."

The temptation for Sarah to keep Marion awake and talking was almost more than she could tolerate, but she managed to control her curiosity long enough for Marion to fall asleep. Sarah left a note for her father to ask if he could make other sleeping arrangements, and she let him know that she would explain later who the stranger in the bed was and how she knew her. Then she returned dutifully to the hospital with a much lighter heart than she had felt in many weeks.

Ted returned home to a dimly lit room and was about to lie down on his bed when he noticed it was lumpier than usual. He at first thought that Sarah had come home early to take a much-needed rest, but he shortly realized that it was not his daughter in the bed. He looked more closely and saw a very attractive young woman, sound asleep. He quietly looked around the room and found the note Sarah had left for him. He sat down in a chair to think about what he could do to help. He knew that Elmer would probably let him sleep on the cot in his office at the stable that he ran, but he did not relish the idea of imposing on him for an unknown period of time.

He decided to go for a walk around Richmond, which he thought must have once been one of the most charming cities in America. At this point in the war, it was overcrowded with all kinds of people, good and bad: refugees and speculators, suppliers and government hangers-on. There were former soldiers who had been wounded and discharged and were not going home but wanted to remain where the center of government was located. Now there were also more active enlisted men who visited Richmond whenever they could because the Confederate army of General Lee was so close by that it was easy for the men to get into town.

Ted was wandering aimlessly around the capital, admiring the beautiful grounds, lost in thought about the changes in his own life during the past three years. He was startled into alertness by a commotion in the distance. He turned a corner and saw a fine-looking young man, dressed in a beautiful gray uniform, openly confronting a woman on the street. As he got a little closer, he recognized the woman as one he had previously seen at Elmer's stable. He had learned that she always seemed somewhat mentally unbalanced, but in point of fact, she was very intelligent and lived in a boarding house where many Confederate government contractors and employees lived. She was so effective at picking up information from overheard conversations that she was an invaluable source of information to the Union army.

As he approached, he recognized the officer who was accosting her. He suddenly stopped, and as he started to slowly edge away from the crowd that was gathering around the scene, he heard the loud conversation between the odd pair.

"Just come with me, Mrs. Steagle, and I will escort you to the proper authorities who can verify whether or not you are a spy. If not, they will tell me that I am wrong," Chauncey Murphy said.

"I just want to go home and take care of my mother," Mrs. Steagle responded.

"I know for a fact that you don't live with your mother," he said. "You live in a boarding house with a number of government employees."

"No, I live in that alley over there in a shack with my aged mother," she said, pointing south toward the river.

Ted could tell that Chauncey was growing frustrated by the spins this conversation was taking, none of which had anything to do with his attempt to take Mrs. Steagle into custody. He had heard that she could turn any confrontation about her real business around in so many circles that most of the men assigned to the provost marshal's office had given up and just left her alone. Besides, at this point in the war, there was little information that either side needed that they could not get by looking through a good pair of binoculars.

Then he witnessed something that startled him and, he was sure, startled everyone else who was watching. Chauncey picked the woman up like a sack of potatoes. With her over his shoulder, he started to walk away toward the office of the provost marshal. But before he got twenty yards, another man, obviously a superior officer, stopped Chauncey in his tracks with a challenge about what he thought he was doing.

"General, I know that this woman is feeding a known agent of the North information about the state of the army defending Richmond, and she has been doing it for most of the war. I've been told that she is not as feebleminded as she seems but is in fact very astute at picking up and transferring important information."

"If that is true, Captain, then have an accusation attested to and then take a squad of men to arrest her wherever she lives, but do not pick up anyone, especially a woman of her years, and attempt to arrest her or harm her in any way. Is that clear?"

Chauncey sullenly saluted and walked off muttering to himself about the stupidity of not hanging spies outright.

Ted arrived a few minutes later at the livery stable and found Elmer busy with paperwork. He was getting ready to forward information about the latest troop movements through Richmond and some statistical estimates that he had put together from information given to him that very day by Mrs. Steagle.

Ted explained first about the young woman he found in the room he shared with Sarah and then quietly pulled Elmer back into the stable and told him about the scene he had just witnessed. "I wouldn't normally worry about that kind of situation, Elmer, except that Chauncey said that he knew that Mrs. Steagle was giving her information to a known Northern agent."

Elmer thought about what Ted had said, and then he said, "Finding that young woman in your boarding house may be a break for me. It gives you a legitimate reason to move in here for a while, and maybe we can use it to transfer the lease for this property to you. I have other agents I can work with here in Richmond, and a couple of them will hide me if the provost marshal starts to get too aggressive."

"Do you think that you have that much time to make your arrangements?" Ted asked.

"I hope so. For now, why don't you get your things, and you can use the extra room next to the office for your quarters. Are you still able to take your meals at your boarding house?"

"I am sure there will be a charge, but yes, I will eat there."

CHAPTER 39
1864, RICHMOND, VIRGINIA

The plan didn't work.

When Ted returned to the livery stable the next day after his noon meal, he found Elmer hanging from a beam in the stable. There was a note tacked to his corpse that simply read, "Hanged, for spying against his own neighbors."

Ted was so shocked that he didn't know what to do. He sat down in the office and contemplated what this would mean to Sarah and anyone else who was working with Elmer. He didn't personally know anyone other than Mrs. Steagle who was working with Elmer. Finally, he decided to go to the police station and report what he had found.

As he walked to the station, he had an overwhelming feeling of sadness. He had only known Elmer for a short time but had grown to respect and like him. They shared a common bond in their love of horses and mules, and he was one of a few people in Richmond that Ted trusted. The fact that he had been so willing to let him use the spare room at the livery stable showed that he trusted Ted too.

Ted also worried about who would have the audacity to lynch a person during daylight hours, especially considering that anyone could walk into the stable at any given moment. His first inclination was to think that Chauncey had taken out his frustration at not having been able to arrest Mrs. Steagle, but he liked Chauncey and could not imagine that he would do something so criminal.

Maybe someone had observed the number of people coming and going in the stable and realized that there was a lot more traffic than would be justified by its normal business practices. Maybe someone was trying to steal a horse or something else. There were a lot of unknown possibilities, especially in a city that had grown from just under forty thousand to over one hundred thousand people in just over three years.

Ted considered all of the possibilities and tried to think of ways he could take over the lease of the stable and maybe continue Elmer's work by changing the pattern just a little. Besides notifying the police, he had an even more urgent need to get word to Sam about the possible danger now facing Elmer's contacts in Richmond.

Ted was so late getting back to the boarding house that he missed the evening meal. Luckily, the owner, Mrs. Young, was kind enough to prepare a light meal for him. Then he went up to the room he had formerly shared with Sarah and asked her to take a short walk with him. She made sure that Marion was comfortable and then met her father in front of the house.

As they were walking slowly together, anyone observing them closely would have seen tears start to roll down Sarah's cheeks.

"I hate this murderous war. I see so many who are dying slowly from wounds that they did not expect to receive. And now you tell me that Elmer was lynched. We may not know who did this, but it wouldn't have happened if our so-called leaders knew how to bring justice without war."

Ted was at a complete loss as to how to comfort Sarah at this moment. All he could do was try to stay close and give her his one good shoulder to cry on. They stood under a large tree for a long time as he let her tears bring a quiet relief to her heart. He was wise enough to not try to say anything.

Finally, as her weeping stopped, he said, "I am worried about Elmer's contacts. If they go to the stable without knowing about his death, someone may be watching to see if they leave without doing any normal business. I talked to the police about taking care of the horses tomorrow and hope that I can prevent any of his people putting themselves in jeopardy. But a bigger problem is that we need to get word to Sam so that he will know that his organization in Richmond is broken."

"There are always boys that need to go back to their homes from the hospital. Maybe I can find some that are from close around Fredericksburg," Sarah said. "Then it would be easy for me to travel to any Union encampment and be 'captured.' Sam thought that would be the best way for us to contact him in an emergency."

"How would you return to Richmond? Or would you go home to Cleveland? Or maybe back to Pittsburgh to wait out the end of the war?"

"I want to come back to Richmond. I have been able to convince a number of young men that when they go home they should stay. I think I can help more by doing that than any other thing. As long as I am not away too long, I believe I would not arouse any suspicion."

Then Ted thought of something he had not told Sarah that he realized he should, even though it might prove painful for her to hear. "Yesterday I warned Elmer that he might be in danger because I had heard a member of the provost marshal's guard confronting Mrs. Steagle on the street. He told her that he knew she was a Union spy and that she had been seeing another known spy. She was not arrested only because the officer's superior stopped him. The member of the guard was obviously angry that his superior officer would not let him take her into custody."

Sarah was surprised that her father had not told her this before. "Why didn't you tell me this before now? It seems to me that we are all now compromised."

"It's worse. The young man who was so angry was Chauncey. I knew that he was responsible for talking you into helping with the Southern cause, and I thought that you might be upset that he is now part of the provost marshal's guard in Richmond and that he is the person who confronted Mrs. Steagle on the street. I am not sure how you feel about him now. It seemed to me that during our hunting trip you were becoming very close."

Sarah now thought very hard about whether or not she should tell her father what she had witnessed almost a year ago, just before the battle of Gettysburg. In the end, she simply said, "I have my mules at the stable, so I will need to pick them up along with my wagon before I leave to notify Sam. Do you think there will be a problem with that?"

"I don't know. I am not really sure how much business they will let me conduct. All the police officer told me was that I could take care of the animals and stay in the spare room at the stable. I know that there will either be a guard there or nearby for the time being."

CHAPTER 40

1864, CITY POINT, VIRGINIA

Sarah was surprised at how easy it was to travel north from Richmond during the last summer of the war. She knew that the main Union force was concentrated at Petersburg with another strong force facing Richmond from the east, and that General Lee had his forces spread thinly in trenches facing both forces. What shocked her was that they only saw one Union patrol on the road they were taking to a little town south of Fredericksburg. She was able to leave her charges at a farm there while she continued north to Fredericksburg where she could telegraph Sam that she would be arriving in Norfolk within twenty-four hours with urgent information.

While Sarah was waiting at the Norfolk telegraph office that morning in early July, she received word from Sam to come on to City Point by the next boat. He had sent instructions to his agent to arrange for her to have a spot on the next steamboat so that she could travel as quickly as possible.

Sam was waiting for her when the boat docked that evening, and she noticed that he seemed to have aged and looked very careworn. As they sat in his office, she started by telling him about the death of Elmer and how her father had found him. "My father also told me to be sure to tell you that before Elmer was murdered, Mrs. Steagle had been confronted just after leaving the stable by a member of the provost marshal's staff. He wanted to make sure that you would hear personally that it was Chauncey Murphy who confronted her."

Sam looked shocked for what seemed like a very long time as he absorbed the news of both his good friend Elmer and his boyhood friend Chauncey, and the possibility that Chauncey might have had something to do with Elmer's death.

When he finally spoke, his words came slowly. "I can't imagine that he would have been murdered by anyone associated with the provost marshal's office. I know Chauncey can be reckless at times, but murdering someone is something that leaves me speechless. I can't believe he would have had anything to do with it."

Sarah's hesitation was profound in the silence. "I know you have tried to find out who I was following before Gettysburg, and I should have told you then. Chauncey was responsible for Marty's death, Sam, and now I feel responsible for Elmer's death because I didn't tell anyone."

Sam could hardly bring himself to face Sarah as he thought about the past year and the grieving his family had gone through. He needed some time away from Sarah to decide not only how to proceed but also (and more importantly) how he felt about being deceived.

"Sarah, I need some time. Will you stay in City Point tonight so we can talk in the morning, please?"

As Sarah quietly left the office, Sam began the impossible task of making sense of all of this news. He did not see Sarah until the day after their planned meeting.

Sarah walked into his office two days later and found him looking completely exhausted and careworn. "Sam," she started to say.

He held up a hand, and for a few moments, there was silence between them. "When you left the other day, Sarah, I left too. I was going to have you held here until I returned from Richmond, after

I had a chance to confront Chauncey. I didn't make it even halfway to Richmond. I started to think about how hard this past year must have been for you. Right now, I can't imagine how you have had the strength to carry the burden you assumed."

Sarah was overwhelmed that Sam had been concerned enough about her burden that he would not complete what she was sure would have been a journey of revenge.

"Marty was my brother. Elmer was my friend. I now know that Chauncey murdered my brother, but did he kill my friend too?" Sam said quietly. "You have been in danger, and it is more threatening now than we may know. Your father is in even greater danger because if he runs into Chauncey, he will automatically be compromised."

"My father and I are not accusing Chauncey of lynching Elmer, Sam. We are more concerned that he knows both of us, and that puts us in danger. We worry even more that our continued presence in Richmond might compromise other agents." She added, "I know that you had become good friends with Elmer, and this must be a horrible shock. I am so sorry we have lost him."

"You know he volunteered for this duty because he had two friends who were lynched near his hometown because they were caught burning a railroad bridge that was used to transport troops to General Bragg. He wanted to do something to help end the war as soon as possible."

"Sam, just in case you are still thinking of keeping me here, I want you to know that I need to go back to Richmond. If you need a little more time to think about what to do, I will stay for a short time, but I will go back."

Sam thought for a few more minutes and said, "Yes, I would like to give this more thought. Most of Elmer's contacts were people he recruited, and even though I have his list of names, I only personally know you and Ted. But there is one other thing you should know. One of Elmer's contacts is here in City Point now and did not tell me anything about his death, even though he left Richmond only a day before you did. The problem is that this man's name is not on Elmer's list. Do you think it is possible that he could have left Richmond without knowing about the murder? You can give that some thought tonight while I try to cope with your news and decide what to do about it."

"Can you tell me this person's name?" she asked.

"Amos Taylor. He said Elmer sent him with special instructions and information for my eyes and anyone I thought could use the information. I passed the notes to my superior, and he will evaluate them along with other information we have been collecting."

Sarah thought for a moment and then asked Sam for paper and pencil. Sam watched for about ten minutes as she sketched, threw away the paper, and started again. "What are you drawing, Sarah? It better not be a picture of me."

"Please look at this carefully. It's been almost a year, and that seems like a lifetime, since I have seen a man named Amos Taylor, but I think this should resemble him."

Sam studied the drawing, and while there was a resemblance, it didn't quite look like the man he had seen just a few moments before he started to talk with Sarah. Then he realized what the difference was. "Can you draw a patch over his left eye?" he asked.

She quickly added the missing feature and when Sam looked at it again, he was certain that they were talking about the same person.

After a moment, Sarah said, "I know Amos Taylor, and the last time I saw him was outside of Chattanooga after I had given Elmer the information about Longstreet's movements. Amos was trying to convince a Southern captain to have me summarily hanged as a spy. This much I know—he had overtaken me on my way back to Chattanooga from Cleveland, and so he might have seen me at Elmer's blacksmith stable. Do you think he is possibly working for the Richmond provost marshal?"

"There are certainly a lot of links in this chain. Maybe we have a possible murderer here that we should hold until we know more about what he is up to."

"I would like to have some time to myself, Sam, but there is one more thing. I believe Amos would have left Richmond after I did because I had to stop along the way to deliver three young soldiers to their families before I got to Fredericksburg."

With that, Sam escorted Sarah back to the steamboat, where he arranged for her to have a cabin. He gave instructions that the boat was not to leave City Point without clearing it with General Grant's staff. On the way back to his quarters, he determined that he would at least have Amos stay another day at City Point while he worked out all of the possibilities that Sarah's revelation had suddenly dropped on him. This had been a very long three days.

CHAPTER 41
1864, RICHMOND, VIRGINIA

Sarah returned to Richmond via the same roundabout route that she used to get to City Point. Amos was allowed to return to Richmond the day before she left. She and Sam hoped to leave him without any suspicion that Sam knew about Elmer's death. The most dangerous information that Sarah carried back to Richmond was the knowledge of the names of Elmer's contacts. Sam knew that he was putting her in jeopardy by giving her complete knowledge of the operation, but he felt that there was no one else he could trust. He did not want to sacrifice the rest of the organization and felt that between Sarah and her father, he would have careful, reliable contacts to carry on the work.

Sarah was worried that she would not be able to do all that was expected of her. She felt a strong impulse to just return to Pittsburgh, far away from fighting and intrigue, to simply abandon her role as the new main Union contact in Richmond. In the end, it was concern for her father that drew her back into the thick of the dangerous work.

The first natural contact she made with him was when she returned the wagon and her mules to the stable. She had timed the return so that he would be closing up and could walk the many blocks back to the boarding house with her. She thought that would be the least suspicious way for them to be able to talk and plan how they would either revive the network or just leave and go home. The second option was never a realistic consideration because of all that they both felt they could accomplish by remaining in Richmond.

"Have you talked much with Marion while I have been gone?" Sarah asked as they walked. It was the first thing she'd said that was not related to spying for the North.

"I have checked with her every day to make sure she was recovering. I was worried the day after you left because she developed a fever, and I was afraid that she might have some infection in the wound. But that passed within two days, and since then she seems to be regaining her strength. She wanted to know if you would be willing to go with her back to her home in Georgia. She found out that you have made a couple of trips to help young wounded soldiers get home safely."

Sarah thought about this and realized that it might be the best way to throw suspicion off of her and her father if she continued to help soldiers return to their families. She wasn't sure if Sam would approve of the plan, but she realized that he really couldn't object if she went ahead without letting him know before she left Richmond. There would only be two people—her father and Ralph Baxter—who would be able to tell him, and neither was likely to do so.

When they arrived back at the boarding house, she immediately went upstairs and found Marion looking young and strong again.

"You look like you could use an extended rest, Marion. What do you think about returning home and taking responsibility for raising that son of yours?"

"Do you think that raising a child is restful?"

"I meant that you need a rest from being in harm's way. I hope that your family does not live too close to Atlanta. That seems to be the direction that the Union army under Sherman is heading. Where exactly is your family's farm?"

"We live on a farm just outside of a town called Perry. It is pretty far south of Atlanta, and I think the nearest railroad passes through Macon. When Edmond and I came north, we were able to travel partway by train, but I don't know if it would be possible to return the same way now."

Sarah wondered how she could check to see what route they would need to take to reach Marion's home. It would be imperative for her to be able to travel by train if she wanted to make the trip. The excursions to reunite men with their families in Virginia were relatively short compared to what faced Marion before she would reach her family.

"Why did you come back, Marion?"

She could see that it made her friend very uncomfortable to talk about what had happened when she returned home to have her baby, but she finally said, "My family and Edmond's family are not exactly close. When I arrived home married and ready to deliver a son, my father didn't want me to have the child in our home. I was completely undone by his attitude. He had always before been so kindly toward all of us. I knew he did not have anything to do with Edmond's family, but I thought it was mainly because they're rich and we're poor. But now I believe there could be something more to it than that. At any rate, Edmond's family took me in to have the baby, but after he was born, they changed completely toward me. They brought in a wet nurse, and then Edmond's mother took both my son and the nurse to live with her family in Savannah. I became so despondent that I came north to die in the war."

"Do you have any idea if they are still in Savannah?"

"I haven't heard from anyone since I left home last November. I am hoping that they have returned home and that they will have softened toward me. I don't know what I can do if they won't let me have my son back."

Sarah was sickened by the tale. She could not comprehend what kind of people would turn out a daughter in need or steal a child from the wife of their deceased son. She had a vivid memory of a question from a dying boy: "Why?"

Her tears flowed quietly along with Marion's as the two of them sat close together on the room's small settee.

Suddenly Sarah's concern about the distance and whether or not Sam knew what she was doing lost all significance. She would go south and do her best to help Marion recover her son, Edmond Nelson.

After dinner, she gave her father a copy of the picture of Amos that she had drawn for Sam and explained about the possible danger in dealing with him. He was unknown to Sam except that he had come through the lines claiming to be a new courier for Elmer. Then she explained to her father that she would travel with Marion, and he made a suggestion that would have profound implications for the future of the Richmond spy ring.

"There is usually more strength in numbers, especially if you have right on your side. If you can find a wounded officer who would be willing to travel south with you and confront both families with the rightness of Marion's cause, then your chances of success will be that much better. I believe that it would be especially helpful if her father could also be persuaded to remember his love for his daughter and join in with the enterprise."

Then Ted went back to the stable and returned just before Sarah was ready to retire for the night. He didn't say anything but handed her a small box before turning and leaving. In the box was one hundred dollars in gold coins. It would be far more than enough to travel on, so all Sarah had to decide was that the remaining balance would be given to Marion to help her.

At that time, there happened to be several high-ranking officers recovering from severe wounds in the hospital where Sarah was working. One of them, in fact, was a general who had been a colonel the year before, the officer who had been so generous with Marion. Sarah decided she would approach him first. It would have been perfect if he had been from southern Georgia, but he was from Kentucky.

When she explained to him what her errand was and who it would benefit and why, he looked incredulous. "I can't believe that any two families could be so callous and mean. Naturally, if you think that I can help, I am happy to go. Besides, it will give me a chance to see the Deep South before this war changes it forever, which it certainly must."

Sarah could not have imagined at the beginning of the journey how it would change the lives of so many people. General Shirtz relished the chance to travel in the company of two young women, both of whom were very attractive in their own ways. Marion was strong featured with blond hair and, when cleaned up, was more than equal to any woman he had ever known. He also knew some of her history with the army and was drawn to her strength of character. He also recognized that, as they traveled farther south, she was becoming more apprehensive about what lay ahead of them.

Sarah, on the other hand, was a beautiful young woman, more so than he remembered from last spring. She seemed to have grown from an awkward teenager to a lovely, brown-eyed, raven-haired beauty. He thought about this as they traveled deeper into Georgia, and he relished taking the side of both of these young women.

The interview with Marion's father proved to be far more difficult than any of the three had imagined. He seemed to be both angry that his daughter would ask to come back to their home and fearful that she actually wanted him to approach Edmond's parents about taking back her baby. The cause was so just that she couldn't fathom why he would flatly refuse or why her mother took his side.

As the three approached the Nelson plantation, a flood of memories, both sweet and bitter, drew almost instant tears from the poor girl's eyes, and they were forced to wait in the long drive to the mansion for her to compose herself.

The plantation was nothing like what General Shirtz or Sarah expected. It looked deserted because the fields around it were overgrown with weeds and the extensive lawn around the home had obviously not been cut for some time. The only real indication of habitation was a large vegetable garden to the side of what must have been the kitchen building. When they parked the carriage at the front porch, a black woman wearing an old-looking dress came out.

"May I tell my mistress who is calling?" she asked.

Marion did not wait for the formalities but jumped from the carriage and burst past the slave into the house before the girl was able to finish her question. With that, the general and Sarah got out of the carriage and went up onto the front porch.

"We came to see Mr. and Mrs. Nelson about Marion's baby. I believe she may already be confronting them," Sarah said.

The maid showed them into the main parlor of the house where they found Marion holding her baby close and weeping quietly. With her in the room was a fine-looking couple of upper middle age, who looked perplexed to say the least.

"My name is Norman Shirtz," the general said, "and I have accompanied these two young women to help further their quest to recover this baby." He stepped forward to shake Mr. Nelson's hand.

"I am not sure how you think you can help, General Shirtz. We sent a letter yesterday to Richmond hoping it would find Marion to ask her to come back home and take her baby off our hands. It seems that she anticipated our desire," responded Mr. Nelson. "Who is this beautiful third member of your party?"

"This young woman's name is Miss Sarah Clarke, and I believe she is the quiet instigator of our enterprise."

Mrs. Nelson spoke up. "My husband mentioned a letter we sent, but I fear it makes us sound like we don't adore our grandson. We do love him but have found that our age and physical condition, plus the loss of many of our people, have made it very difficult to care for him properly. In that letter, we invited Marion to come and live with us for as long as she cares to. We would really not like to be separated from little Edmond."

All three of the travelers looked astonished at this surprising turn of events, which none could have anticipated. Marion was so taken aback by the offer—and the sudden turn in Edmond's parents' attitude toward her—that she was speechless.

Seeing this, Sarah spoke up for her. "I am sure that Marion would like to stay, but not having anticipated this, I am afraid we are all left a little breathless."

The most surprised was the general, who had harbored dreams of figuratively coming to the rescue of Marion and her son and, by doing so, finding favor in her eyes. He had never told either of the young women that he had been widowed before the war started, or that on this long, circuitous journey, he had become enamored of Marion.

"Mother, I believe it is time for us to invite our guests to share what little food we have and to spend a few days with us as we all get used to a change in our household."

"Oh yes, please. We have food and plenty of space. Please feel free to stay as long as you wish. General, you look like the journey may have been very difficult for you. Would you like to rest? Or we have a hot spring house that you may find very refreshing," offered Mrs. Nelson.

With that invitation, the group settled in for what unexpectedly turned into a delightful stay.

CHAPTER 42

1863–1865, GEORGE WASHINGTON LEE

I t had been so long since George Washington Lee had arrested Chauncey in the spring of 1863 that he was amazed that the war had not ended. The war, for George, had been one disappointment after another. He did not immediately receive the assignment he wanted—to be assigned to a unit that would see quick action.

He at first enlisted in an infantry unit that was commanded by white officers, and the unit became part of the standing army that was kept close around the capital to protect it from Southern invasion. When the fighting took place in Gettysburg, George was standing guard duty at the capitol building. He had secretly hoped that Robert E Lee would attack Washington so that his regiment would be needed to really fight.

Finally, in late June and early July of 1864, the opportunity George wanted finally came. The South's General Early led his army through Northern Virginia into Maryland and then turned for Washington. All of the military available in Washington was placed in a defensive line to the west and south of the city, and George was finally able to aim his musket at Southern troops and fire. It was so gratifying to him that he could at last actively do something that seemed important and useful.

That confrontation lasted only a short time because General Grant sent reinforcements from around Petersburg. Then General Early retreated to the southwest, and that ended, for a short time, George's combat experience.

After the fighting around Washington, George was finally transferred to a cavalry unit. He had hoped that he would have that opportunity the previous year and had used the horse Chauncey donated to him to learn to ride. He was not immediately proficient, but when he was transferred to the cavalry, it was because he told his new commanding officer that he knew how to ride well enough to teach other recruits. Even though this was somewhat of an exaggeration, he was given charge of half a dozen new men with instructions to teach them.

He learned a couple of lessons from this experience. The first was that the teacher learns more than the student, and he would be more careful in the future about claiming to know more than he did.

During the winter of 1864 and 1865, his unit did a lot more training than combat. But there were several small engagements with Confederate cavalry that tested his men and their skill in life-and-death encounters. George had been wounded at a place called Woodford, which was almost on a direct line between Richmond and Washington. His cavalry troop had been riding patrol when they happened on a small patrol of Confederate cavalry.

The Confederates were in the area trying to pick up men who had gone home on leave from the hospital in Richmond and had not returned to the army. They were working with men from the Richmond provost marshal's office, and Chauncey Murphy was along as an observer.

Chauncey did not recognize the young Negro lieutenant who went down with the first volley because he and his men turned and retreated when the Union troops pressed the confrontation and drove them off. George was picked up and taken to an aid station in Fredericksburg where his wounded leg was treated.

Fortunately for George, he was sent home to Philadelphia where his mother was able to nurse him until he was able to return to duty in March 1865. By then his cavalry unit had been reassigned to General Sheridan, and George had been replaced by a white officer. When he went back to duty, it was with an infantry regiment facing Richmond, commanded by General Weitzel. Everyone was getting ready for the winter rains to stop so that the roads would dry out enough for the Union to begin their spring offensive.

CHAPTER 43

1864, RICHMOND

The first chance Sarah had to speak to Ted was late the day after she returned from the Deep South. She had been gone for just over three weeks and had a great deal to tell him. As they sat in the stable visiting, she explained first about the social part of the visit and how really good Edmond's parents had been to Marion.

"I don't think we will see her back in Richmond before the end of the war unless it is to come here to marry General Shirtz."

Ted looked astonished. "Why would that happen?"

"It's the fastest proposal that I have ever known. I think he was impressed with her at their first meeting because she had the strength to fight even though her husband had just been killed and she was pregnant. He was very kind to her last year, and when he heard that she had returned and been wounded, he was more than eager to help her recover her child. You should have seen the look of disappointment on his face when he found out that he would not need to plead a strong case for the return of the child to his mother. I think he had prepared a very persuasive argument and wanted to show Marion just how strongly he felt. Anyway, by the third day, the Nelsons recognized that he was in love with Marion and encouraged him to ask for her hand."

"What about her parents?"

"They had already cut so many ties with Marion that when General Shirtz asked for her father's permission to marry, the man really could not object. But he did seem pleased enough that she would be marrying a general."

"Well, that is the damn'est proposal I have ever heard tell of."

"There's more. When General Shirtz and I were traveling back, he was telling me that if Sherman took Atlanta, which it looked like he would do, then the Confederacy was finished. He was returning to serve on the Richmond military staff of the Secretary of War, but his heart was not in it. He is afraid that the members of government do not really realize how badly off the rest of the country is. As we were talking, he said he wished there was something he could do to help hasten the inevitable. I was nearly going to try to recruit him to give us information, but I thought better of the idea until I had a chance to talk with you. Do we still have an active group of agents in Richmond?"

"Barely. Ralph has been sent with only one message asking that we wait to send any information until they can evaluate how to proceed. I now suspect that Elmer was murdered by someone who knew nothing about his spying activities. I believe that Amos knew of his death but was just trying to find out from Sam who might be recruited as the new leader in Richmond. In fact, he may have been naïve enough to think that Sam would ask him. One thing is for certain—we will not use the stable as a front anymore. Part of the message that Ralph gave me was that if I wanted to use it just as a normal business, I should go ahead, but Sam thought that it was too compromised to be useful anymore as a center of operations. We can contact Ralph with anything of vital importance through the mother of Mrs. Steagle. She is not on Elmer's list but is known to Ralph and Sam. They call her Mrs. Land, but her real name is Olivia Landeach."

This took more than a few seconds for Sarah to process, and it made her wonder if Mrs. Landeach was also encouraging wounded men to go home. She finally asked, "So are we waiting to hear from Ralph?"

"Yes. I have decided, however, to continue to lease the stable. I find that many people come through here with more information than they realize. It is quite easy to piece together bits of information and make a fairly good conclusion about the shape of the armies around Richmond. It reminds me of the information that you gather from the wounded coming into the hospital."

"That's true. No one person gives a complete picture, but all of the soldiers talk about where they have been and where they think the hard fighting will be next."

With the end of the conversation, they discussed how to stay in touch with General Shirtz and decided that, if he were moving from the hospital to a boarding house, that Sarah would know about that and they would try to get Ted a room at the same place.

It all seemed very easy while there was a slowdown in the fighting around Richmond as the Union army tightened the siege of Petersburg and Richmond. There was still a continual stream of wounded and dying coming into the hospital, but the rate had slowed to the point that it was just demanding and not overwhelming. Sarah had a little more time to visit with some of the soldiers, and she encouraged them to go home to recover. She was always sure to teach them about the necessity of keeping their wounds clean and dressed. She would also let them know that it would be better to stay away from people carrying contagious diseases and that would increase their chances of surviving their wounds.

Everything she said during these times with the men was a subtle means to decrease the number of Confederate men available to fight. Her long-term hope was that those who were recovering would decide, on their own, to stay home for the remainder of the war. She would never be sure how effective this hope was, but she did know that over two hundred men left the hospital to recover at home. She had been able to transport twenty-five of those herself from the time she delivered her first group to Temporary until the end of 1864.

During the late fall and winter of 1864 and 1865, Sarah and Ted grew close to General Shirtz by visiting with him at the boarding house where he and Ted had been living. He was not very talkative about his responsibilities in the war department, but he was more than animated when the talk turned to the end of the war when he would travel to Perry, Georgia, and consummate his courtship of Marion. His love for her had held fast during the time since they had parted in the late summer. He would read parts of her letters to him concerning young Edmond and the work on the plantation but then stop abruptly when the letters became more personal in nature.

A change occurred in February that signaled heightened preparations for a spring offensive that was sure to come. Sarah knew about it privately because she had made three trips to the North to deliver more boys into their families' care and then gone onto City Point where the buildup of men and material was so obvious that she was sure that the Confederate general, Robert E. Lee, knew about it. This was confirmed one evening when she and Ted were having dinner with General Shirtz.

After the meal, the three of them stepped out onto the porch where the general could have his evening cigar. He started to talk in a very low whisper. "I know that I shouldn't be talking about this to anyone outside the war department, but a most distressing note was sent to President Davis from General Lee. He referred to his knowledge of the Union buildup along their lines, and he wrote that he also knew of the vast depot of supplies they have at City Point. He told the president that when the offensive comes in the spring, he doesn't think he will be able to hold the lines protecting Richmond. He said that he would try to give enough notice if the government wanted to evacuate, possibly a week, but his army was so thinned out by desertion and death that he had less than half the effectives he would need for a realistic defense."

Both Ted and Sarah sat for a few moments in stunned silence, not because of the news of what was happening in the Union camp, but because this was the first significant information that General Shirtz had ever shared with them about the progress of the war. And it showed the thinking of the commanding general of all Confederate forces.

"The only reason I tell you this is that you may want to think about leaving Richmond before the war starts up in earnest in the spring."

Sarah looked at the two men and finally said, "Do you think that the hospitals will not be needed as much then as they have been in the past? I don't see how I can leave without feeling that I have fallen short of my duty."

Ted thought for a few moments and then said, "Naturally, I will stay wherever Sarah is. She is my only family. What do you think will happen when the army leaves? Will they leave behind any kind of force to enforce law and order?"

"We haven't started to plan for any evacuation yet. We were only just informed of the note to the president."

"Would the government surrender, or do you think they would evacuate?" Ted asked.

"I am not sure how they would function if they evacuated. They would not have any way to communicate with all of the armies throughout the South. It would be a nightmare to try to coordinate any effective resistance to the Northern offensive." With that statement, General Shirtz realized that he had said more than he intended and quickly changed the subject back to more mundane topics.

CHAPTER 44

1865, RICHMOND

When Sarah and Ted got together the next day, they talked about the conversation and General Shirtz's startling revelation. Their first object would be to let Sam know, since it told much about the thinking of the Confederate leaders. It was an admission from the highest authority that the numbers of men available to fight for the South were tremendously decreased. They had been so many months without any solid information about the Southern army or General Lee's intentions about standing and fighting or retreating, or for that matter attacking. Now they knew, at least, that he would not try what was in his view a futile defense of Richmond.

"Do you have any more men that you can take home to the North?" Ted asked.

"I'll need to check at the hospital. There haven't been any for over a month. But maybe I can encourage someone to go home."

"This work becomes more dangerous as the days go by. Even though the information we give can be logically deduced, there are people who are desperate enough that they would take the law into their own hands and punish anyone they think has wronged them. I hope I don't need to remind you about caution."

"I've been threatened enough to know to watch my back and my sides."

Sarah was able to round up four young men that she could take north the following week. The weather was so rainy that the mules had a very hard time pulling the wagon, and the going was very slow. At times, Sarah thought that she would need to turn back and try to get the information through to the Union army another way. Finally, a week after leaving Richmond, she was able to leave her passengers on a plantation outside of Fredericksburg and then travel on to the river.

The only problem with the entire trip was the uncomfortable feeling that someone back in Richmond might have been watching her or Ted and guessing what they had been talking about, or even possibly overhearing part of the conversation. With so many people living in Richmond, it was hard for Ted and Sarah to have a private conversation without looking suspicious.

When she arrived in City Point toward the end of March, the weather was starting to turn warm, and the roads were drying out. This was an obvious time that the armies would start to move, and so she felt an urgency to let Sam know that General Lee was not planning an all-out defense of Richmond.

After she had given all the information that she had accumulated to Sam, he realized that this could be the last time he would see her before the war ended. He couldn't imagine that the South could resist longer than the end of spring.

"Sarah, the information you have given me today will help in the planning for the end of the war. It is the most valuable news since the intelligence you gave us at Chattanooga. But I need to tell you that I have been worried about you these past several months, more than you could ever know. When you left here the last time, I had an impulse to ask you to go to Pittsburgh where you would be safe, rather than returning to Richmond. Now would you consider not going back to Richmond?"

Sarah thought for a few moments and then said, "I would be happy to go to Pittsburgh if I could be sure that my father would be safe. I still think I can be of some use to some of the men who are injured and maybe help some get safely home."

"So I guess you are telling me that you are going back to Richmond, even though without the army there, it will be more dangerous than you can imagine?"

"Yes, I want to be with my father. If he decides to leave, I will go with him."

"Did your contact tell you anything of the plans to burn government warehouses in the city? We have been hearing rumors about it for weeks now but have had no verification."

"We have been hearing the same rumors, and I am sure that they are well based, even though there has been no official announcement, probably because they are afraid of how people will react."

Sam was trying to prolong the visit as long as he could. He had started to tell her how he felt about her, but he lost his courage because he was sure she would not reciprocate his feelings. Instead, he started to talk about other, more mundane issues. He had become so fond of her that when he said that he had been worried about her safety, it was because she was in his thoughts constantly. Now she was about to leave again, and he was not able to say what he felt.

As he watched the riverboat leave the dock, he could only hope that she would be safe and that he would be able to see her again. He felt the hollow feeling that comes when contemplating a missed opportunity and a lonely future.

CHAPTER 45

1865, OUTSIDE RICHMOND

E ven though George Washington Lee's hopes to be part of the actual fighting had not materialized the way he had envisioned, he
was happy to be where he was in March of 1865. He had indeed maintained the rank of lieutenant when he transferred into the Twenty-
Fourth ACT Regiment of the Union army, in spite of the wound he
suffered at Woodford. There was a tension among the men that came
from having been idle for most of the winter as they awaited the offensive that would surely come in the spring. Now, there was excited
anticipation that they would either attack Richmond or be attacked
as the Confederate army tried to escape the trenches they had occupied since the summer of 1864.

The men had talked anxiously as they were given information
from those who had been watching the Rebels prepare to receive a
strong attack by placing new land mines and abatis to slow down any
attacking troops. The men's tension now grew because they could all
feel the near end of the war, and they were all desperate to survive
the coming battles.

George knew that if they were ordered to attack against such a well-prepared defensive position, the casualties would be high. That knowledge was not exclusive to the few officers who were in charge of the strategy, but the common soldiers were well aware of the difficulty because they would be the troops responsible for carrying out the orders to take the Confederate capital.

Because General Weitzel understood how his men felt, he hoped that there might be a last-minute political surrender by the South. He had orders from General Grant to try an attack if it seemed like he could surprise the Confederates enough to limit the number of casualties, but it was left to his discretion whether or not to proceed.

CHAPTER 46

1865, RICHMOND

The people in the city of Richmond had been on very short rations for most of the final winter of the war. Sarah was hard-pressed to provide enough food for her father and herself. The boarding house they lived at still charged the same amount for room and board but had stopped providing an evening meal each day. The morning meal was likely to be some grainy mush and maybe a piece of bacon, if they were lucky. The talk of the soldiers at the hospital changed over that winter and took on a note of desperation as their rations were cut to the lowest point in the war. The only subject was whether they would have enough to eat to fight on.

Many people wandered the streets during the day just looking for a scrap of food that would supplement the little they had at home. Sarah had stopped using the stable to board her mules for fear that some desperate person would think that they looked good enough to eat. She now kept them on a small farm about three miles outside of Richmond. Even there, it tore at her heart whenever she checked on them because they looked so starved.

As the weather started to change at the end of March, Ted and Sarah listened every day for the booming of cannon that would signal the beginning of the end for the South. Knowing as they did of Lee's intention to quit the defensive works around Richmond, they wanted to be on their guard for any sign of evacuation.

They were alerted on the last Saturday of March when General Lee ordered an attack against Union-held Fort Stedman, part of the line the Union army occupied east of Petersburg. The sound of that battle carried to Richmond, as if it were a very distant thunderstorm. Since it did not continue, Sarah decided that it was not the push by the Union that she and her father had been expecting. They learned later that General Lee had hoped the attack would buy a little time for the Confederacy so that he could determine when the Richmond defenses would be abandoned. It did not work. The fate of Richmond was still dependent on drying roads and the strategy of the Union general.

CHAPTER 47

1865, RICHMOND
SARAH'S WAR ENDS

Jefferson Davis wanted to put off to the last minute his order to pack up the government and leave the capital. He had sent his wife south before the spring offensive started and probably should have followed her sooner than he did. He waited until Sunday, April 2, when he received a note from General Lee. The note stated that because the Union attack had begun in earnest, he would be forced to begin evacuation of the lines around Richmond that very day. He suggested that President Davis leave with the government as soon as possible.

That began the most confused, terrible day that the war had wrought on the beautiful city. Part of the fault lay in the decision by the city fathers to destroy the large quantities of liquor in the city; part of the fault lay in the decision to set fire to any military stores that the army could not evacuate; and part of the fault lay with Mother Nature, who on a whim blew up a mighty wind storm.

The result was that a dangerous fire, spread by a harsh wind, destroyed the heart of the business district, and hundreds of drunken looters added to the danger and confusion. For many people, the only safety was to gather what personal items they could and go to the nearest large open space they could find to await a dreadfully anticipated tomorrow. The Confederate army was pulling out that Sunday night and would leave the city unoccupied before dawn Monday.

George Washington Lee was in Richmond early on Monday, April 3, 1865. He and his men were quickly assigned to help citizens suppress the fires that had destroyed so much property. One of the few compliments that the citizens of Richmond ever gave the Union military occupiers of Richmond was that they had worked hard to put out the fires and quickly establish order.

Ted and Sarah had been at the boarding house, which had not been threatened by the fires, waiting just as anxiously for any news of the running battle now being fought by Union and Confederate forces. Early Tuesday morning, they decided to make their way to the stable to see if it survived the horrific fire and to check to see if there were any horses or mules left. They were both quiet as they walked the two miles east to the edge of the burned-out part of Richmond. There they found, to their surprise, a partially burned structure that had somehow lost its face without losing its body. It contained one broken-down horse. Attached to a ceiling beam was a note that read, "Thanks for the horses, which the Southern army needs more than you. Please send this note to President Davis. I am sure he will reward you generously." It was signed "A. Thomas, Staff Sergeant, Richmond Defenders." He'd added a PS: "Please accept my personal mount as partial payment."

The personal mount had been on very short rations for a very long time and looked ready to expire if it was not fed very soon. Sarah went to a nearby stall and found a pitchfork, which she used to rake together a little dried hay to give the starving horse. Then she carried a bucket of water from the tank and put it in the trough. Hopefully, this would help the horse survive one more day.

Sarah found her wagon was intact, but the gold coins were gone, and she couldn't remember if she had told anyone where they were hidden. The large pistol Ralph had given her was still under the seat where it had been ever since it was used in a place called Temporary. As she remembered more of the past, she realized she had given most of the coins to Marion for her and her young son Edmond.

As she and Ted were quietly talking about the past, a loud voice from behind them said, "See, Amos? I was sure they would show up here."

They quickly turned and saw Amos Taylor, still dressed in his butternut uniform, leveling a musket at Ted. The person who had spoken was dressed in civilian clothes and looked very familiar. He spoke again. "You should remember me, Sarah. I recruited you to come along and join with Amos, Clarence, and the recruits. We traveled a long way together."

Immediately, they recognized Chauncey, even though he had put on what once passed for fine clothes and had a hat pulled low over his forehead. They realized that he and Amos must be desperate to get away from Richmond, and that they were dangerous because of their fear. Amos looked like he had participated in the looting, because a fancy pair of woman's shoes was dangling from his bedroll. They would have made him look comically ridiculous, except for the musket pointed at Sarah and Ted.

Sarah had started to edge around to the side of the wagon where she could reach her revolver when Amos said, "I believe she is looking for a big horse pistol in that wagon, Chauncey. I believe she was planning on shooting me outside of Chattanooga when I caught up to her after she left Cleveland."

Chauncey immediately started to search the wagon and found the large Colt. He aimed it at Ted and said, "You better hitch up the wagon to that horse. He doesn't look like much, but I bet he could at least get a couple of 'poor farmers' far enough out of town to make an escape."

"You'll be lucky if he makes it through the barn door," Sarah said.

"Help Ted with the hitch, Amos. He won't want to see his child damaged," Chauncey said as he trained the pistol on Sarah.

They were just finishing up the hitching when a voice from behind Chauncey said, "I believe I have the pleasure of placing you under arrest for a second time."

At the sound of the voice, Chauncey whirled and pulled the trigger of the large gun just as it came in line with George Washington Lee's head. There was a hollow click as the hammer came down on an empty chamber. Chauncey could not have been more surprised and angry when he saw that surrounding him in that small stable was a squad of Negro soldiers, appearing even blacker because of the soot from the fires they had so valiantly fought.

As Chauncey was being made a prisoner, Sarah could not resist telling him that she had emptied the pistol after the killing in Temporary of a young man not that different from himself. He also tried to live through lying and cheating. Then Sarah took the glove off her mutilated left hand and held it up for Chauncey to see. She said to Lieutenant Lee, "This man mangled these fingers making his escape after murdering a very young Union courier outside a little village named Gettysburg. I hope that you can have him put on trial for that murder."

At first, Ted was surprised that Sarah had finally named her long-ago assailant, and then he was very proud of her for confronting him with the evidence of his brutality.

Then Sarah asked George, "How do you know who he is, and who are you, and why did you say you were arresting him for a second time?"

George looked at her. "I recognize him from an encounter we had outside Falmouth before the battle at Chancellorsville. I gained a horse from him when he suddenly left our guard shack. He's even wearing the same suit of clothes. He's just a bit older. We saw him and this man dressed as a Confederate soldier trying not to be seen, and that looked suspicious. I decided to bring my men as I followed them."

Sarah was looking at the men—Ted, Amos, Chauncey, and George—but seeing other faces that she knew and loved. The tears started to flow down her cheeks as sacred memories flooded her heart.

Ted watched her carefully and then quietly said to her, "Sarah, it's time for us to go home."

THE END

Made in the USA
San Bernardino, CA
09 September 2015